KING SCRATCH

Jordan Krall

For my family

CONTENTS

6

PROLOGUE

The stray cats outside were making a racket but Jim didn't mind. Those furry little bastards loved to hang out in the hallway right outside the door to his apartment. They would meow through the night, waiting for Jim to open the door, let them in and give them some water or, better yet, some glazed donuts.

Tonight, however, Jim was too busy to take care of them. He was entertaining a woman, a small-time actress named Peggy Entwistle. She had pursued the career for a few years but only landed a small role in low budget mystery that did poor at the box office. It didn't matter to Jim, though. She was a sexy broad eager for attention and he was giving it to her one inch at a time.

Little did Jim and Peggy know that a man named Black Boned Keith was across the street, watching them from his apartment window. But little did Keith know that something was watching *him* from somewhere in his apartment building.

The whole world: a crude but complex series of voyeuristic actions.

From the hallway, Jim could hear the grey cat making pigeon sounds.

"Oh, hell, I'll do it," Peggy said, pulling herself off of Jim's dick. She grabbed an empty pot off of the sink, filled it with water, and opened the door to the hallway. The cats, seeing Peggy's face, scurried like mice. "Oh, well." Peggy shut the door and walked back to Jim.

Across the street, Keith took out a matchstick, sniffed it, and then inserted it into his urethra. It was unpleasant, yes, but it reminded him about life. It reminded him of what the world really was: a crude but complex series of familiar but uncomfortable insertions.

PART ONE
TIP-TOE THRU A CAR CRASH

"Thrice did I slip backwards into strange forms of myself, and thrice did my Soul save me..."

Austin Osman Spare

"And it shall come to pass afterward, that I will pour out my spirit upon all flesh; and your sons and your daughters shall prophesy, your old men shall dream dreams, your young men shall see visions..."

Joel 2:28

CHAPTER ONE
Jim

I was fucking Peggy when the phone rang.

This happened way before Peggy went out west to worship that huge Babylonian sign out there in Hollywoodland. It was before she committed suicide by jumping off that very same sign so she was still in one piece. And what a piece it was. Blond hair, breasts like immaculate bubbles and perpetually sweaty skin I wished I could lick forever. For a small-time actress, she was pretty sexy.

I listened to the voice chirping through the phone while I stared up Peggy's nostrils. Her breasts flapped to their respective sides as she still quivered from my wet insertion. The person on the phone belonged to Red Henry, my mentally ill ex-father-in-law.

"It's not my fault, no, not my fault!" he shouted. I had no idea what he was talking about. I never had. Periodically he called me to babble on about something or another. Sometimes the calls lasted one minute while other times they lasted thirty. I was too nice of a guy to hang up. Most times I just half-listened while reading the paper.

"Red, Red, listen. I'm busy right now," I attempted to get through to him as I gave Peggy a slurping thrust. Her nostrils were wider, like dark, hairy pennies. I smelt the smudged copper aroma and saw Abraham Lincoln himself shudder from my penetration. I was John Wilkes Booth, pulling out of Peggy's axe-wound and putting a milky white bullet through Lincoln's crown.

"Jim, Jim, I have too great a soul to die like a criminal!" Red Henry shouted over the phone as I bled my manhood into Peggy as she snorted and gagged. Her nostrils coughed like Lincoln and then turned black, rusting into shadows of Lyndon Johnson.

I spoke through my post-coital exhaustion. "What? Red, you're not a criminal, take it easy." He didn't answer me. I'm sure his mind was still racing, skipping past the hundreds of women's shoes he's sniffed and then chewed on. I can imagine Red scratching at the pimples on his chin as he counted curls in his pubic mound.

"I have to go, Red. Call me back later, alright?" I waited a few seconds and then heard a moan of agreement. I hung up the phone.

Peggy sat up. When I looked at her face covered in blotches of milky goo, I searched around for a tissue, thinking she had a runny nose. Then I remembered the seminal assassination.

"You okay?" I asked.

"Yeah, of course. Like I haven't done anything that before," she replied with a condescending laugh-cough. I handed her a tissue but she waved it away and used her forearm.

Though Peggy would end up dying in L.A., we were far, far away from the glitzy latrine of that showbiz world. We were in a tiny, pay-by-the-week apartment in South River, New Jersey. I had a room above a bar and I was constantly serenaded by a cacophony of voices, clanking glasses, and muddled music at all hours. After about two days, the soundtrack was like a soothing ocean, lulling me to sleep with the occasional yelp of "Rack 'em up, bitch!" or "Yeah, I fucked her".

As Peggy was putting on her bra and panties, I wiped my penis with a pillowcase. There was a smell in the room, something like flowers and feces, not totally unpleasant. Peggy was carefully putting on her pantyhose when the phone rang again.

"Yeah?" I said, assuming it was Red.

"Jim, is that you?" It was my ex-wife, Laura. I didn't even know she had the number. In fact, I asked the landlord to put the phone in for me two days before. Cost me an extra seven bucks a week. Local calls only. But it was worth it.

"Yeah, it's me. What is it, Lore?" I asked, gently but playfully spanking Peggy on the ass.

"My dad just called, he's freaking out. Did you talk to him?"

"Yeah, I just talked him. He was rambling on. You know how he is." I tried to sound annoyed.

"There's someone at his house. I heard voices in the background and he didn't sound right. Something's wrong. Did he say anything to you?"

"Yeah, just the usual stuff. Honestly I wasn't listening, I was busy."

"I'm sure you were," she said. "What's her name?" She was taking her role as the wise old mother figure again.

"None of your goddamn business." I said, not really meaning it. I really wanted to brag about Peggy. I wanted to impress my ex-wife with the top-notch pussy I was getting after our divorce. *Hey Laura, I creamed this girl real good. A real looker. She's younger than you, too.*

"Well, can you please just go by his place? I'm leaving now, I'll meet you there." She sounded like she didn't care about who I was with anymore. That bothered me. I wanted to tell her. *Christ, Laura, you should see Peggy. Areolas like two little fried eggs. Tasty!*

"I dunno, maybe." I was tired and honestly didn't think Red was in any danger.

"Just go there, please," Laura pleaded and then hung up.

"Goddamn," I said, slamming the phone down and watching as Peggy sat on the nightstand, smoking a cigarette. I could see up her skirt.

I quickly got dressed while convincing Peggy to go along with me. She agreed and we got into my car, a souped-up beast that I drove when I ran moonshine out of the Pine Barrens.

As we made our way through the next town and headed for Old Bridge, Peggy counted the matchbooks on the dashboard. There was a time I had collected them. I don't know why. Though I tried to start a conversation on the ride over, she just kept counting.

"89, 90, 91....." she said and that's when we hit the deer.

CHAPTER TWO
Black Boned Keith

Keith put his binoculars down. He had watched as Jim and Peggy left the apartment and hopped into that loud rust-bucket that Jim called a car. Keith stood in front of the window, naked.

He swayed from side to side, his flaccid penis a pendulum with a matchstick peaking out. Keith got a cigarette from a crumpled pack on the windowsill and put it between his lips. He grabbed the pack of matches and then grabbed his member. With a half-smile, Keith flicked the tip of his penis against the matchbook. He bent down and lit his cigarette. The lit match then fell to the ground as Keith waddled to the other side of the room, puffing smoke as he went.

The smoke lingered around the floor and crept up the walls, disturbing the squid. It slid out from underneath the bed, riding on its own juices. It fluttered at Keith's ankles.

"I told you, Smitty. This is my last pack, I promise," Keith said, puffing on the cigarette. The squid leaned to one side as if to say "I don't believe you," and then slid back underneath the bed. Keith heard a sound like a tape recorder being rewound.

He opened the door to his apartment and listened. In the hallway, Keith could hear the yapping of televisions, radios, and bedsprings. The girl in 2A was begging for junk again, pleading and crying to someone over the phone. Keith imagined the girl's dealer coming over to bring the heroin. The girl shoots up. The dealer, clad in black leather gloves, uses a straight-razor to split her skin. Hundreds of intersecting lines bleed, criss-crossing until the girl's flesh resembles Christmas ribbon. The dealer-assassin leaves her dissected body on the living room floor and walks out of the apartment.

His daydream was interrupted by an odor of shit that appeared like a ghost, slowly making its way past Keith's nostrils. It's probably that asshole next-door, Keith thought. The man in the next apartment was a weirdo who dressed up like a baby and hired prostitutes to play the part of mommy. On several occasions, the baby shit his diaper and the mommy of the day refused to change it and left the apartment, shouting obscenities.

Keith walked out naked and stood in front of his neighbor's door. He pounded his fist on it.

"Open the goddamn door, asshole," Keith said. He heard a whimper, a squishing sound and then a wooden thump. "Christ, at least clean up the shit," he said, this time raising his voice. The smell of the man's shit made Keith's penis and balls shrink. He imagined the man-baby sitting in a playpen, brown leakage on his thighs and a thumb in his mouth. A bloated prostitute in her mid-forties lay strangled to death on the couch. She had refused to change the diaper and so the man-baby threw a tantrum, strangling mommy to death while he sucked on his brown thumb.

Keith knocked again but got no response. He turned to go back to his apartment when he glimpsed someone down the hall. They were hidden in the darkness, the light bulb having burned out weeks ago. The person was tall and Keith could see something shimmering. Was it jewelry? A knife? Keith leaped into his room and locked the door behind him.

CHAPTER THREE
Jim

The car was totaled.

My head was caught in the steering wheel. Peggy was next to me, unconscious, tongue hanging out of her mouth. Smoke rose up from the front of the car like a fog. I got myself free and staggered out. Surveying the damage, I knew my bootlegging days were over. There was no way I could afford to get the car fixed.

The deer was mangled so badly it looked like it was part of the car. Pieces of glass and metal were embedded in its body as it trembled. The poor thing was starting to make me sick so I walked around the back of the car and pulled Peggy out. She woke up and vomited.

Peggy's pantyhose were shredded from my dragging her to the side of the road. I stared at her legs and for a few seconds I wanted to put my nose up to them and sniff. I guessed they would probably smell like sweat, nylon and asphalt.

"Jim, what happened?" Peggy said through vomit-spittle.

"We hit a deer. Car's wrecked," I said. Peggy's vomit was now a small pond of chunky, green-purple sludge. I smelt it from where I was standing.

"I think I need an ambulance," she said softly, gagging.

"Okay." I walked over to the road. I stood there ready to flag down the next oncoming car. I saw headlights in the distance, coming down fast.

I waved my arms in the air. The car pulled over and a door opened. Out stepped a black man in a tattered suit. He took a few steps and then whistled.

"Quite a crash. You okay?" he said, a huge grin covering his face.

"Yeah, I think. I don't know about her though," I said, walking over to Peggy.

"Those damn deer come out of nowhere," he said. His hands fiddled in the pockets of his tattered trench coat. I nodded while nudging Peggy awake.

"Would you mind giving us a ride to the hospital?" I asked.

"No, not at all. Just give me a second." He walked back to his car. He started taking things out of his backseat and putting them into his trunk. I grabbed Peggy and helped her to the man's car.

"Howdy, miss, real sorry about your accident," the man said. Peggy nodded.

We all got in the car. I noticed that the man had shaving cuts all over his face as well as ugly stubble. I realized I didn't introduce myself. I could almost hear my dad's voice saying *"Jimmy, be a gentleman."*

"Oh, by the way, my name's Jim," I extended a hand.

"Hi Jim, I'm Fred," he replied and shook my hand.

"I really appreciate this. I just hope she doesn't get sick back there," I said, glancing at Peggy who was looking green and ready to burst.

"Aw, it won't matter much. There's been so much disgusting shit in the backseat, no one would know the difference," Fred laughed. I looked over my shoulder and tried to imagine the disgusting shit that Fred mentioned. Images flooded my mind. Twenty-dollar whore excretions smeared with lipstick and moist cocaine. I envisioned some sort of semen-fueled Black Mass, filth and fuckery to the sound of prayers chanted backwards. Pentagrams drawn in black shoe polish on the sweaty, nervous back of a virgin hitch-hiker.

When Fred laughed I noticed that he was missing some teeth on the right side of his mouth. It was creepy and made me think he was going to go ahead and bite something, maybe my face or Peggy's. He had a glimmer in his eye I didn't like.

"You know where the hospital is, right?" I asked. I wanted to make sure the trip was going to be as direct as possible.

"Sure do, on Main Street, by the donut shop," Fred assured me. Meanwhile, his smile lingered for a few seconds longer than I thought necessary. I noticed he didn't blink but instead just stared straight ahead to the point where I was expecting his eyes to start watering. They didn't.

Fred's hands on the steering wheel were starting to quiver a little but he didn't seem to notice. I looked back at Peggy who was in an accident-induced stupor. I nudged her and her eyes opened wide but I could tell she didn't know what the hell was going on.

"Quite a piece of pussy you got back there," Fred said, turning his head. His unblinking eyes faced me while his hands still shook. I got nervous.

"That's a little out of line, Fred," I said, not wanting to start trouble. Again, my dad's voice: *"It's best to use a man's name when talkin' to him. It makes him feel at ease, like you give a shit."*

"My apologies, Jim. But let's be honest. It's mighty unkind of you to not offer some of that cunt-cake. Hell, she's half out of her mind. She wouldn't know the difference whether it's my dick or yours, you know? Just sayin', since I'm givin' you a ride and all."

I'm the type of guy that tries to avoid trouble when possible. I try to prepare for trouble, sure, but I make my best efforts to avoid it. Rarely do I have that macho attitude that gets a lot of men into trouble. Instead, I usually pick the choices that will cause me the least complications in the end.

"Seriously, Fred, that's not funny," I said.

"I'm not trying to be funny," he said. "I'm not a fucking comedian, Jim." That's when he took one of his quivering hands off the wheel and grabbed my neck. I've never felt a grip like that before. It was a serious vise grip and there was no way I could pry it loose.

So I grabbed the knife out of my boot and stabbed Fred in the chest.

Call me paranoid or whatever but I like to be prepared so I always carry a blade with me.

His blood splattered all over the steering wheel. He let go of my neck and made gurgling sounds. I pulled the knife out of his chest and into his glassy right eye.

The car swerved but I caught the wheel in time, managing to step on the brake and pull it to the side of the road. I reached over, opened the driver's side door and pushed Fred out. Once I had stabbed his eye socket, he wasn't much in the mood for struggling. He just whimpered, burped and surrendered to Fate.

I got out and pulled Fred to the back of the car. I opened the trunk and realized that there might not be enough room for my new cargo. The trunk was full of brown leather satchels. I got curious, opened one up and almost vomited from what I saw: a battered corpse of an infant complete with bite marks.

CHAPTER FOUR
Black Boned Keith

Keith put on some clothes. He kept an ear out for the potential intruder in the hallway. Contemplating using the fire escape to avoid any confrontation, Keith instead settled on charging out the door like rhino. It wasn't his usual style, but something about that person in the hallway gave him an ache in his bowels.

He was wearing his usual drab outfit: a beige button-down shirt and dirty black jeans. Keith wasn't interested in fashion because he'd rather be naked. Now he was holding his hand over the doorknob, getting ready to rush out into the hallway and down the stairs.

Out the door Keith ran, flopping against the wall of the hallway, hurting his right shoulder in the process. He heard his door slam closed behind him. A shuffling sound soon followed as he fumbled down the stairs. The shuffling turned into a pair of high-pitched whispers. They followed him down as he almost tripped down the darkened stairwell. Keith's heart was beating fast and he was starting to sweat. The whispers that followed were scaring the shit out of him.

He finally landed on the sidewalk outside, moonlight hitting his face like a frying pan. The whispers didn't follow him outside. Keith heard a shattering noise hit the door and then go back up the stairs. Nervously he walked past the Mexican restaurant wanting to step inside and check out the sexy Spanish woman but decided he wasn't up to it. He needed to get a cab and intercept Jim and that whore Peggy.

The street was bustling tonight. The drunks, hookers, and junkies were in full force. Keith eyed the prostitutes. Most of them dressed in sweat pants and dirty shirts with football team logos on them. All sorts of stains were evident: motor oil, semen, salsa, baby food, and an assortment of unknown substances. They weren't just hookers. They were desperate women at the end of their rope who sell their orifices daily for dope money. But Keith was never interested in them. He liked his women to have all of their teeth left in their head.

Keith passed *Ram's Head Bar & Tavern* and had to talk himself out of going in for whiskey. He had given up moonshine months ago and now only drank legit liquor even though shine was quicker and cheaper. Keith knew he had to quit after he found himself standing face to face with Abraham Lincoln himself, the president's skull popped open like a soda-pop can. Lincoln had stared at Keith who watched in horror and awe as the silent Lincoln turned into a very talkative John Wilkes Booth. Keith couldn't understand most of what the man said except for the last part. Booth grabbed Keith by the ears and shouted: "I have too great a soul to die like a criminal!"

The next morning, Keith poured three gallons worth of shine down the drain.

CHAPTER FIVE
Jim

The way I saw it I could do either one of two things. First, I could ignore the totally repellent shit in Fred's trunk and drive on. Only problem is that I knew in good conscience I couldn't do that. It seemed to me Fred was a degenerate child-killer and that I couldn't ignore. My other choice was to go to the police station and report my findings. That, too, didn't strike me as something I could do. After all, I did just kill the son of a bitch. Granted I did the world a favor by wasting Fred, I doubted the cops would see it that way.

I decided against ignoring the contents of the trunk. I knew if I left the car on the side of the road, I wouldn't be able to sleep unless I forced myself to discover the deep, dark secrets of Fred's car. Instead, I settled on first taking Peggy to the hospital and then going to Red Henry's house. After that, I would deal with the whole dead-infants-in-trunk situation.

Every satchel in Fred's trunk had a battered and bitten infant inside. I moved some of the bags to the backseat, not telling Peggy what was inside. I heaved Fred into the trunk, his one good eye staring at me, glassy and wide like a speckled marble.

Fred's other eye was missing, its socket a deep red that reminded me of seedless strawberry jam. It was actually less creepy than the other eye, which kept staring up at me like a marble. Before closing the trunk, I found myself entranced by the empty socket. I bent down and inspected the messy abyss. Images of my days as a short-order cook shuffled into my head. There was a guy who always came in on Saturday mornings, a guy named Keith. He would always order the same thing: corn pancakes with a side dish of strawberry compote. I remember one particular morning. I was preparing the order and started to stare at the bowl of red mess. Cathy, one of the waitresses, shook me out of my trance.

"Hon, whatcha up to? That boy is waitin' for his pancakes," she had said, lipstick on her teeth as always.

"What? Oh yeah, it's ready, sorry," I had muttered, not sure why I was having images of an empty red eye socket when I looked into the bowl. The corn pancakes looked fine. In fact, they actually looked so good that I was almost ready to eat them myself and just make Keith wait a few more minutes for another batch.

Cathy took the food out to Keith and I could see by his face that he was pissed as hell. He was the type of guy who'd force himself to not enjoy a delicious meal just so he could complain about it afterward. I wasn't in the mood for that kind of shit that morning but I knew Keith was a regular so I had to deal with him.

The only reason why I even knew that guy's name was because he seemed to make every effort to tell the waitresses that he, Keith, thought the pancakes were too burnt or the eggs too rubbery. At first, my reaction was "Who the fuck does this guy think he is?" but then I realized that he was just another lonely flake who needed a routine. So be it.

Saturday after Saturday, Keith and I developed a sort of long-distance relationship with Cathy or another waitress bringing messages back and forth. He'd complain about the food and I'd send back a semi-sarcastic apology along with a three-day old slice of pie. Most of the time he wouldn't respond but he always ate the pie, though I knew he knew very well it was stale.

My relationship with Keith didn't end there but I wasn't thinking too much about it while I was looking at Fred's gooey socket. I actually started to think about that waitress Cathy and the way her ass stuck out against her skirt. She was an older woman, with puffy blond hair and a lot of wrinkles. Her breasts jutted out like droopy hypnotic doorknockers. Many a mornings passed when I dropped a spatula as she walked by. I tried flirting with her once but I had a feeling she thought of me more of son than a screw-interest.

As I stared down in the trunk I started to smell Fred's urine and shit and I had a vivid memory of the time I walked in on Cathy going to the bathroom. Her white panties were around her knees and she was in mid-wipe. I stopped short and her eyes widened in embarrassment. I was a little bit embarrassed but I was more entranced by the sight of her shapely legs and her ass bulging over the toilet seat. Our eyes met and for a second I swear I had an opening where I could've seduced her. Then that opening was gone and I apologized and walked out, the scent of her perfume and shit lingering in my nostrils.

I closed the trunk and went into the driver's seat. Peggy was out like a drooling light. The car sped off and I drove in the direction of the hospital. Wanting to break the silence and get my mind off all the fucked-up shit that had happened so far, I turned the radio on and listened as some drunken man sung the blues, going on about some broke down engine wheel.

The car started to shake and smoke. Then it stopped in the middle of the road like an exhausted elephant.

CHAPTER SIX
Black Boned Keith

Keith jogged down Main Street until he got to Brewer's Taxi Cabs. He almost tripped when he got there, his green scuffed boots scraping against the pavement. He smelt cigarette smoke and dog shit at the moment he stood eye to eye with a cabbie who had just gotten out of his car.

"Hey, I need a ride," Keith said, both anxious and apprehensive. The cabbie was all muscles and beard hair.

"Sorry, I'm not on duty," the cabbie replied. He put his hand to his chin and fiddled.

"Anyone else around? I need a ride."

"Yeah, someone should be here soon. Where you headed?" the cabbie said, plucking out a small beard hair that resembled a spider leg.

"Fisherville," Keith said. He was sweating now. His left eye started to twitch. That was always a bad sign. His thoughts now went back to the intruder in the hallway. Even after catching up with Jim and Peggy, he was going to have to deal with whoever –or whatever- is up there when he got back.

"You kidding me? You can fucking walk there from here." The cabbie shook his head. "Ahh, fuck it, I'll drive you." The cabbie laughed and spat out a yellow glob of after-dinner phlegm.

Keith nodded and hopped into the backseat. The dog shit smell was getting stronger and with it was the stench of pond scum. The cabbie, Keith noticed on the license attached to the dashboard, was named Matthew O'Kelly.

They drove off in silence, Keith listening to the gurgling digestion of Matthew's stomach as well as the metallic settling of the car. About a minute into the ride, he looked up and noticed Matthew looking at him in the rearview mirror.

"I was just looking at your tattoo. What is that? Snakes?" he asked. Keith looked down at his chest and realized that his shirt was not buttoned all the way.

"No." Keith reluctantly pulled down his shirt a little more. "It's a squid."

"What the fuck is it doing? It looks like it's eating a brain." Matthew's eyes bugged out of his head and the car swerved to the right in order to avoid another car.

Keith said, "Yeah."

"Weird. What you into, anyway? You a squid-fucker or something?" Matthew seemed on edge. Keith got the feeling that Matthew had some strong opinions on squid.

"It's hard to explain…" Keith tried abandoning the subject. He turned his head to look out the window. Matthew didn't seem that keen on the idea of dropping the topic.

"You think I'm too goddamn stupid to understand some fucking tattoo?" His voice echoed in the cab, making Keith's ears pop.

"Calm down." Keith raised his voice and immediately realized it was probably a mistake to do so.

"Don't tell me to calm down. I had too long of a day to put up with some bum's fucking bullshit." Matthew's face was red now and he turned his head, facing Keith eye to eye.

Meanwhile the car was moving and Keith could see a tiny bit past Matthew's head as the headlights guided them through the darkness. As the cabbie spit a few more words of anger into his face, Keith noticed a dark shape getting bigger.

"Watch out!" he said, pushing Matthew's face forward, the beard hairs causing friction against his hand. Keith rubbed it against the seat of the cab but ended up getting his hand wet.

Like a cannonball, the cab hit the back of the car that was stopped in the middle of the road. Matthew put his arms up to protect his face from flying glass but ironically, the windshield did not shatter. Instead, the collision forced Matthew's seat backward until it was crushing Keith's left leg.

The car that they had hit was an accordion of metal and glass. As Keith shouted in agony, he stared out at the wreckage in front of the cab, wondering if anyone in there was sharing in the pain perhaps as some sort of universal and communal nerve-ending experience.

Matthew was leaning back on the seat, looking upside-down and sideways at Keith. He was pale and breathing heavily.

"Goddamnit, I can't move," he said while his seat was crushing Keith's leg.

"Get up…" Keith said, "move…."

"Don't tell me…" Matthew said right before he vomited. It hit Keith on the right leg. Chunks of chicken and corn collected on the floor mat.

Keith struggled against Matthew's weight, attempting to pull his leg out from under the seat with minimal damage. He was having limited success since Matthew was turning back and forth, causing the seat to dig deeper into the area above Keith's knee. The actual kneecap was being pushed down so much there was an audible pop every time Matthew moved back.

Grimacing, Keith opened the door and lunged out. His right hand hit the asphalt hard and his elbow failed him. He hung from the car, twisted at the waist, his left leg still not loose. Keith's eyes bulged in pain and his eyelids dropped slowly. Matthew coughed up another batch of chunky vomit and passed out.

Keith was in a haze of vague pain and increasing numbness. His eyelids fluttered and then opened. Crevices of black tar lay before Keith: jagged revelations of burnt rubber and road kill. The tiny asphalt hills turned into towering mountains inhabited by a tribe of primitives. They spent most of their day meditating on the highlands until ethereal shapes and sensations became all they experienced.

Though the primitives would have no conception of the significance of this fact, the forms they saw often took the shape of rusting cars. The rust would flake off and combine with the black snowflakes that flew off the top of the tar-mountains. Keith himself did not see this swirling combination but instead sensed it through the eyes of a half-burnt primitive who gripped the rib bone of a goat while in a trance.

Keith kept his mind's eye on the shivering hands of the primitive man who was now holding up the bone in front of his face. Flakes of rust and snow fell down around him, forming a shimmering car. The two ends of the rib bone twisted to form a circle and the primitive held it like a steering wheel. Fingers and bone trembled while unblinking eyes stared out past the snow-rust windshield. The mountainous land of black tar became a busy highway of transcendental mind projections. Primitive people of all ages, shapes and sizes were floating around on faded forms of pseudo-automobiles that glimmered and hummed as they glided through the crevices.

As the space before Keith became crowded, his mind started to superimpose a memory over the proceedings. Entranced mountain people spiritually convulsed alongside a group of masturbating men. The oldest of the group stood in the middle, directing the others. One of the primitive trance vehicles collided with the man in the middle: black snow and rust enveloping hormone-riddled skin. The man put his hands to his face in an effort to brush the phantom glass away. He cried out for his mother as the other men looked on in confused horror. A couple of the men ejaculated despite their terror, the reproductive system ignoring the fear that was circulating in their brains.

Another scene appeared, hanging on the aura of the black mountains. A Halloween many years ago: Keith dressed as Abraham Lincoln. He held a semen-stained pillowcase in preparation for the trick-or-treating. On his feet were his mother's black boots. She told him they looked just like the ones Lincoln used to wear and Keith believed her. He started out the door and down the driveway, hoping to avoid the inevitable. His luck ran out. The door to the cellar slammed open. His father came up behind Keith.

"Lincoln, eh? I guess I'll go as John Wilkes Booth, then," his father had said. A hard knuckle-slap landed across the back of Keith's skull followed by deep alcoholic laughter.

The asphalt below him stood out like brail and he stared at the road below reading it with his fingertips. Keith's nerves shivered and he became aware once again of the crash around him. The front seat creaked and his leg came loose. He fell forward, the warm road like a comforting bed. Keith let out an involuntary sigh. Matthew muttered some curses and vomited on the stick shift.

Keith surveyed the road around him and noticed there were no passing cars. Silence enveloped the stretch of road like an uncomfortable blanket. He crawled over to grass on the side of the road and urinated. The piss splattered on the grass so loudly that Keith became worried about waking any animals that may be creeping in the outskirts of the woods.

As he turned to limp back to the car, he noticed another car about 300 feet back on the opposite side of the road. Its front end had been smashed by what looked to Keith like a mangled piece of deer. He stepped a little closer and then the sizzling heat of recognition fell over him: *Holy shit. That's Jim's car!*

But where the hell was Jim?

CHAPTER SEVEN
Jim

My first thought was: Just my luck.

My second thought was: Peggy's heavier than she looks.

I assumed I'd have to carry her out of the car because she didn't look in any condition to walk on her own. Her chin glistened with yellowish saliva. I quickly got out of the car and started to drag Peggy out. She moaned as I loaded her up over my shoulder and started walking.

For a second I debated pushing the car to the side of the road so I could unload the contents of the trunk. Instead, I decided to take one satchel and leave the rest of them next to Fred's corpse in the trunk.

After I grabbed one of the bags, I walked past the car, balancing Peggy on my shoulder and praying that a car wouldn't drive past while I was hauling an unconscious girl into the woods. That would look suspicious to someone who was coming in mid-scene.

I managed to walk about a half a mile with Peggy until I had to go into the woods and rest. I gently laid her down and then collapsed from exhaustion onto a pile of branches. I closed my eyes, wanting to melt into the ground, to become one with the grass and the dirt and the crooked twigs. I was so worn out from the crash I could feel my back sink into the soil. My head was swimming in a heated pool of moonlit sweat and pine-scent. As I meditated on the insides of my eyelids, I heard Peggy moving in the grass. She made a purring sound and then coughed. The cough caught in my ears, vibrating the

swayed as if caught in an aural hurricane.

des of my head itched so I rubbed them against the

cat when it has had a good dose of catnip. The sharp

edges of twigs scraped my temples and then I remembered something I was told when I was a kid: if you are hit in the temple too hard, you die. I never found out if it was true or not but it always scared me growing up. I'd always worry that if and when I got into a fist-fight that the other guy would go for my head: a sucker shot right to my temple, killing me and robbing me of the chance to counterstrike.

That's what I was thinking as I heard Peggy's cough rush through my ears like the echoes of a waterfall and I scraped the sides of my head. It would have been easier to use my hands but they were at my sides, sinking into the ground, joining the earthworms and spiders in an orgy of peaceful, earthly contemplation away from the non-organic curse of the glass, metal and concrete society that plows its way above ground. I was enjoying my small plot of open space as I sunk into it, serenaded by Peggy's coughing.

My eyelids trembled from a ripple of vibrations. At first, I thought that I had accomplished the task of burrowing myself underground and was listening to the roar of an underground river. Then the vibrations got louder and morphed into an orgasmic spurt of crushed metal and rubbery friction.

The black screen of my eyelids flipped into a dotted green-blue canvas that swayed like the hair in my ears. My body floated up to the surface, a battalion of trapdoor spiders popping out of my pores, crawling their way back to their old homes. I was left feeling like a conspirator with a heart and mind full of secrets.

I became aware of what had happened and rolled over to shake Peggy awake. When I did so, she was already staring out towards the road.

"Accident," she murmured, pointing with a limp hand.

Normally I would go and make sure everyone was all right but under these circumstances, I didn't think it was such a great idea. By the looks of it, someone had hit Fred's car and it was going to be hell trying to explain why there was a trunk full of dead bodies, one of which I was responsible for.

So I grabbed Peggy's hand and dragged her deeper into the woods.

I knew the area quite well since I used to know someone who worked in the clay pits nearby. Well, not worked in the legal, taxable sense but he put in quite a few hours a day bootlegging and to me, that's work.

It took a minute or two to figure out exactly where I was in relation to the cabin. We started walking slowly because Peggy was still pretty out of it. I was too, to tell you the truth, but I was used to pushing myself past the limit of normal exertion. After ten minutes or so, we reached the beginning of the clay pits where the brick industry of the town was born. Now it looked like a wasteland, two square miles of hilly, barren land made of clay. You had to be careful walking through it since there were still soft patches where you could get stuck. It wasn't exactly quicksand but still a hell of a pain in the ass to deal with.

I knew the best way through it so I held Peggy's hand and walked with her through the darkness until we reached the other side of the pits. I was hoping that my old pal Joe Gurney was still living in his makeshift home but I wasn't getting my hopes up. I hadn't heard from him in a while. It had been more than a year and a lot of shit has happened since then but I assumed that nothing in his life has changed and that he'd still be there, organizing his bottles of moonshine for illicit distribution throughout the central counties of New Jersey. There was, however, a good chance he was doing time up in Rahway. Either that or he was blind and delirious from a bad batch of shine. I could just imagine that: Joe half-naked and covered in crabmeat and squid goo babbling to an imaginary jury made of invisible clay.

Peggy and I reached Joe's shack. It had been built into a small clay hill using pieces of plywood and tree trunks. I called Joe's name out but heard no response. Peggy looked dazed but started to come around once I opened the door allowing the stench to hit us.

Moonlight came in thin lines through cracks in the walls. The floor had been made using wooden planks and under it was holes dug out for storing shine and other contraband. Once our eyes adjusted to the dark we saw that the floor, table, and bed were covered in crab shells, matchbooks, squid-guts, and broken glass. The whole place had a warm, fishy, earthy smell that really dug deep in one's nose and

I know from experience that it's a stench that's hard as hell to get out of your brain. Peggy started to cough.

"Goddamn it, Jim, what the hell are we doing here?" she asked, her voice scratchy.

"I don't know. I thought my friend Joe would be here. Doesn't look like he's been here for a while, though. Shit," I replied, flipping through an old, moist issue of a women's wrestling magazine.

"I'm hurt, I need to go to the hospital," she rubbed her neck. "What happened to that guy? I thought we were going to get a ride."

I didn't know what to say. I knew I could tell some of the truth, that Fred had wanted to fuck her and that he had some messed-up shit in his trunk. However, I decided it wouldn't be a wonderful idea to tell her what ended up happening to Fred.

"Fucking guy turned out to be a pervert, wanted to mess with you. I told him to let us out." I lied pretty well.

She looked shocked as if she knew that while she was unconscious, she had escaped a terrible, sleazy fate. Then her eyebrows went up and she smiled.

"Aren't you my little hero?" she cooed and rubbed my cheek. I didn't know what to make of it. Women were confusing to begin with but Peggy, shit. Peggy was one for the record books.

"Hero? I didn't do anything. I just told him to let us out. He was just a horny, old man who thought we were swingers. No big deal," I said, not sure why I wanted to play down my role as protector.

"Yeah, yeah, sure," Peggy laughed and then got serious again, "but really, Jim, this place fucking stinks. Are we leaving or what? Your friend isn't here. And I thought we were going to check on your dad."

"He's not my dad. He's my father-in-law. I mean, he used to be." Like it mattered. "Yeah, we're going to do that just give me a minute to think," I said, trying to sound fed up even though I loved it when women were pushy.

At that point, I wasn't quite sure about our game plan. The night and its events had pushed us to a very unexpected route. Nonetheless, it all started with Red Henry.

I had actually met Red before I became acquainted with his

daughter. It was when I lived in Fisherville. He was my mailman and every afternoon I'd hear his loud, rambling voice as he walked up the street, being friendly with my neighbors. At first, it annoyed me but then I realized that it was his way of avoiding the persona of a messenger. Instead of being a guy who had a shitty, monotonous job delivering to people who never looked their mail carrier in the face if they could help it, he became the daily highlight of his route. Kids liked him and adults couldn't help but smile when they heard him coming. Soon I was having short but meaningful conversations with Red about everything from sports (he liked baseball, I liked boxing) to children (he had three; I didn't plan on having any).

It was a year after being my mailman that he mentioned Laura, his daughter.

"You know, my little girl Laura just graduated from college," he said while handing me a phone bill and some junk mail.

"That's really nice, Red, I'm real happy to hear that. What'd she major in?" I asked. Whenever he had talked about his daughters, I always pictured them as little girls in pigtails. Even though he had previously mentioned their ages, it never dawned on me that they were full-grown adults. I guess that's how much I was stuck in my own little world.

"Psychology. Real smart girl, she is. Takes after her mom of course. Me, I never could figure but my own mind let alone other people's," he laughed.

"Oh yeah, I hear you loud and clear. Seems useless trying to figure people out," I said.

After hearing that little tidbit about Red's daughter, I was a bit intrigued. I had always liked smart girls and psychology seemed like a real smart thing for a girl to be interested in. I made a subtle yet determined effort to get more information on Laura and eventually talked Red into setting up a dinner date. It went well and we were married two months later.

Peggy's heavy sigh dragged me back into the present and for a minute, I saw Laura's face on Peggy's body. What a combination. Laura's face was fuller as was the rest of her body: wide hips, thick thighs, heavy drooping breasts all topped with the most beautiful red hair you've ever seen. A beautiful Irish lass if there ever was one. Peggy, on the other hand was a pale matchstick. Attractive, yes, but not as jaw-dropping as Laura.

I shook my head and my left ear rattled: a bean in a tin can sound that made my lobes itch. For an instant, my nose became my dominant sense organ as the thick, fishy stench continued to force its way up my nostrils. Peggy meanwhile was crouching down, her annoyed sighs still not ceasing as she urinated. Her pantyhose were hanging off her legs, shredded and torn.

I could barely see the piss on the floor but I smelt it. It wrapped around the squid and crab smell like a warm yellow glove. I thought that maybe the combination would be a good perfume. It wouldn't serve the typical consumer, I know. It would surely have a more *discriminating* audience. I saw the small dark puddle on the floor get bigger as Peggy's vagina continued to hiss in relief: the snake at the base of her spine in a drenched fury, its acidic venom spiraling out through Peggy's golden canal in a wet splatter of sacred geometry.

"You're pissing," I said, not sure why I felt the need to state the obvious. We both knew she was pissing but for another instant I saw the whole world embedded in that act. Her liquid would surely leak down pass through the cracks of the floor and into the soil. Insects would be caught in the cascade of Peggy's flood. They would be washed away deeper into the earth, their tiny almost non-existent insect brains never able to contemplate the source of their removal because of the deluge. Peggy's hissing stopped for a second and then started again but this time in short squirts that were accompanied by forceful bursts of air from her ass. She looked up at me and gave me a half smile and a wink.

I squatted down and pulled up one of the floor planks. Below it was a hole filled with jars and bottles. I picked one up. It was half full.

"What the fuck is that?" Peggy said, wiping herself with the cuff of her shirt.

"Moonshine," I replied, shaking the jar.

"Yeah, but what's *in* it?" she made a disgusted face. It was the type of face that would've turned me on if she had done it during sex. But otherwise it was very ugly and unbecoming.

"Squid." I had forgotten that this particular recipe of moonshine wasn't well-known outside of the customers who drank it.

"That's fucking disgusting. Don't you dare drink that," Peggy said. In response, I pried the crusty top open and let some of the liquid splash into my mouth. It was followed by Peggy's dry heaving. The moonshine itself was freckled with squid-skin. As the drops slid down my tongue I recalled the first time I drank this particular recipe.

It had been back when I was running shine. Joe and I were in his shack, smoking and planning the next run when we heard a pained squeal from outside. I walked outside and saw a short, freckled-face man kicking a kitten around like a soccer ball. I ran over to the guy, ready to land a punch on the man's head. Then Joe ran out, passing me like a track star.

Joe's elbow landed on the guy's jaw, making a crunchy sound like nutshells cracking. Once I caught up with him, I followed with a kick to the kneecap, snapping it backwards. Joe kept punching, half-drunk and all-pissed. The kitten was safe but it was squealing and meowing so I picked it up.

I went inside, caressing the kitten when I noticed that it carried a strong fishy odor. I wrapped it in a blanket and waited until Joe came back. He opened up a jar of shine, smiling and waving it back and forth. Then we drank some, went outside and dumped the beaten and battered asshole in the woods. Meanwhile, the kitten was too far gone to survive. The poor thing's stomach had been cut open and one of its legs left raw. Blood caked the top of its head. It was so thick that it raised the fur like a crimson crown.

At that point, the shine was getting to me. Heat burned through my skull. My sinuses became magma. I looked down at the dead kitten. In the grey fur of the animal, I gently brushed a new doctrine that would become my philosophy, my own king's law. With my throat, chest and eyes burning from the shine, I mapped out my future. It was there, written in patterns with thousands of grey hairs like primitive calligraphy.

Joe Gurney and I buried the cat in the corner of the shack. We both said our own separate, silent prayers. It was the least we could do. Afterwards it took a lot of willpower for me not to go back to where we dumped the guy and finish the job.

However, Peggy knew nothing about that shit and I didn't think she cared that much about my past anyway. She was muttering as I finished the liquid contents of the jar along with some chewy bits of old squid. I threw the jar back down into the hole and then started digging up the kitten.

"What the fuck you doing now?" Peggy said.

"Nothing, just shhh.." I couldn't get the words out clearly, "ssshut up."

After thirty seconds of digging, I pulled up the remains of the animal still wrapped in the blanket. Peggy was looking over my shoulder as I opened it up and looked down at the unrecognizable jumble of bones and hair clumps. I looked closely at it to see if I could make out any of my doctrine in the hair but had no luck. I stuck my fingers in the pile and dug around. Moonlight caught something under the skull. A penny, Lincoln side up, was on the inside of the cat's cranium. I grabbed it with my fingers but it wouldn't budge. It was as if it had been glued on the bone. Lincoln's face winked at me.

"Whoa," I said.

"What the fuck, Jim?" Peggy said, obviously seeing what I was seeing. She backed up, almost tripping over an old can of tuna fish.

The moonshine was really getting to me. I could feel it. My palms were sweaty and the heat was spreading from my head to my chest, hugging me like a squid on fire. Along with the fishy potpourri of the shack, a copper smell arose from the kitten's remains.

There was a rattle at the door. Peggy put her eyes to the cracks of the wall to look out. The door opened and a pair of arms grabbed Peggy and pulled her out into the night. I heard her muffled cries as she was dragged through the dirt. I dropped the cat bones and ran out, my head still full of warm dizziness.

A pair of black-gloved hands were holding Peggy by the neck and pulling her across the clay. I ran forward a few feet but stumbled, my chin landing on the ground. My tongue was tightly clamped between my teeth. My consciousness waxed and waned as I watched Peggy being raped by a man in a stovepipe hat.

CHAPTER EIGHT
Black Boned Keith

Keith inspected Jim's car. In doing so, he pocketed several things: about a dozen matchbooks, a half-full pack of Lucky Strikes, and tube of bright red lipstick.

He walked to the front of the car and looked at the twisted deer carcass embedded in the grill. Keith put his hand out and started stroking the deer-fur until it was covered in swirls and shapes on the parts that were not covered in blood or cut open.

A cough sounded from the cab and Keith watched as Matthew fell out of the driver's seat. Chunks of vomit were dripping off his chin as he attempted to pull himself up. Keith strolled back to the cab and bent down next to Matthew. The cabby's face was black and blue, his beard caked with puke. Short, straggly hairs splintered out from the sides of his face. Keith stared at them: spider-legs waiting to be plucked and squeezed between the index finger and the thumb.

Keith rubbed the beard with his knuckles. Matthew cursed.

"Fuck you doing?" he said, pushing Keith's hand away. Keith responded by tearing a spider-leg out, then another. He twisted it between his fingers and put it up to his eyes. He became hypnotized by the sharp ends of the legs that were crusted with flaky skin.

Matthew tried to get more words out but instead let loose a long stream of trauma-babble. Keith continued to pull hairs out of Matt's face. The cabbie squirmed and swung his arms in a weak attempt to stop the abuse.

Standing up, Keith twisted the black, crusty legs between his fingers and dropped them to the ground. He walked over to the car the cab had hit. Its trunk resembled an accordion. There was no one inside so Keith went through the car, pocketing a lighter and a pack of guitar strings.

He went back to the demolished trunk and started to wedge it open. A staggering whiff of rotten flesh and copper hit his face like a stale slap. Keith peeked inside and saw a group of hairy knuckles sprinkled with brownish blood. The knuckles belonged to a hand that was lying on top of soiled leather. Keith's face puckered in curiosity and disgust. He managed to get the trunk open enough to inspect the rest of the contents.

Though he normally would have just stole the satchels right from under the corpse, Keith was dumbstruck at their grotesque contents.

"Jesus Christ," he said. "Dead babies." He immediately thought of his neighbor dressed in a diaper. *The world's a fucked up place*, he thought.

Keith looked in the glove compartment. He found a pocketknife, some toothpicks, a matchbook, and the registration to the car. The name wasn't familiar but the address was.

One of my goddamn neighbors, Keith realized, recognizing the less than prestigious South River address. He didn't recognize it so it wasn't the guy in the diaper or any of the other dregs he knew. He pocketed the registration and started walking down the road, hoping to either hitch a ride or catch a taxi.

He held his thumb out even though there wasn't a car in sight. Several bright stars were visible in the night sky so Keith held his thumb up to cover them. Keith gained double vision when he looked at the sky beyond his thumb. His one solid hand became two translucent ones. The pale cosmos appeared in his skin and his left leg started to hurt again.

He couldn't believe he was still standing. Keith heard the stories about how drinking that moonshine for a long period can permanently dull one's nerves so much that agonizing pain was numbed to near extinction. There even was as story going around about one guy who drank so much of the stuff, he didn't go to the hospital after some junkie stabbed him in the face five times. His eyeball had hung on his cheek for two days until he choked to death on an apple.

Putting his thumb down, Keith started walking toward the inner heart of Fisherville. Through the night air, he smelt the dry, earthy smell of the clay pits. It reminded him of Jim. The thought burned in his stomach as he limped his way down the road. Fifteen minutes later he heard the sirens behind him stop at the scene of the accident.

As the pain shot up and down Keith's leg, he took a matchbook out of his coat pocket and opened it up. He tore a match off and stuck it into his left ear, cleaning out the wax. Then he looked at the address scrawled in spidery handwriting on the inside:

Red Henry
71 Price St

Keith smiled and smelt the head of the match. The wax and sulfuric scent brought three-dimensional images into his mind: fluid-saturated scenes of orgiastic copulations in the midst of wet rocks and seaweed. He sees Jim's ex-wife Laura put her face to the ground, her ass up in the air awaiting insertion, pantyhose hanging out of her anus like a nylon tail. She barks like a dog and digs her face into the sand. Each cube-like grain of sand enacts its own assassination attempt on her pores.

A bone-white squid slithers out of the water and wraps itself around her torso like a diaper. It swallows the musty pantyhose and inserts a tentacle into her aching brown cavity. Laura's head comes up out of the sand, raw and pockmarked from the gritty assassinations. She had inhaled some through her coke-burnt nostrils and the tiny assassins were attacking the inside of her skull cavity with prehistoric glass-rifles.

Keith inserts his penis into her cheek. Now, chipmunk-like, Laura squirms and bucks her hips while the squid-diaper forces itself deeper into her colon. Remembering that he left a matchstick inside himself, Keith slides his hand down his penis in order to work the match out. After several attempts, he succeeds and the matchstick slides out of his urethra and down Laura's throat, which was now paved with stale, stringy drool.

She chokes and lets out a wet and muffled mucus cough. Her mind leaves the abuse brought on by both squid and man. She focuses on the future. She thinks of Jim and the knife-scars spread across his back. An abrasive chill shoots up her spine as Laura thinks of the call she made to Jim. She smiles and looks up at Keith. His teeth are chattering. A moist Pall Mall falls from his lips and lands in Laura's hair. Her fiery red strands tackle the tobacco like the tentacles of a squid until brownish flakes spread throughout the top of her head. They sizzle and remind Laura of shamanistic vibrations and frequencies that her brain translates into images: Keith having a test taken for a sexually transmitted disease. The doctor shoving a Q-tip into his urethra. Keith being shocked at first but ending up enjoying the raw movement.

Keith looked at the address once more and put the matchbook into his pocket.

"Ah, memories," he said, blowing smoke out of his mouth.

CHAPTER NINE
Jim

I'd never witnessed a rape before and it was more disturbing than I'd expected. My mind felt like it was in a hazy, cotton bubble and I think that made the experience even worse.

As the man in the stovepipe hat made violent pelvic thrusts in the general direction of Peggy's crotch, I saw he was trembling like an epileptic. His fists flapped towards her face and blood ejaculated from Peggy's nose. The man turned his head back and forth and then back towards me. That's when I recognized him.

"Joe," I said. I wasn't sure if it was really him or if I was just superimposing my friend's face on the head of this letch. After a few seconds of keeping my eyes on the man, I decided that it was, indeed, my friend Joe Gurney. He pulled his grey pants down and continued to force himself on Peggy.

I regained some of my composure so I crawled over to where the action was and pulled Peggy out of Joe's hands. Joe was grunting, drooling and making other wet noises with his mouth and nose. His drool was grey and shimmered in the moonlight like slobbery diamonds. This slop started to drip down from his eyes, too. I began to notice that something wasn't right about Joe. Physically, I mean. Getting up to my knees, I was at eye-level with his ass.

His ass-crack was covered with a whitish greasy substance and hanging out of his anus was what looked to me like the head of a squid. My fluttering mind brought to me images and memory-scents that made me tremble.

The squid head pushed in and out of Joe's hole a few times and then I heard Peggy whimper and vomit while she crawled away. Joe turned his whole body to me and made a face that lead me to believe that he was searching his brain trying to recognize me. After a few seconds of us staring at each other, he smiled and grabbed my hair.

At this point I was drowsy and my head was full of things that would make a normal person drive a screwdriver into their skull. Joe's fingers became a group of thirteen women surrounding me, their steaming urine cascading down my face and chest. The liquid stained my skin a bright gold and I was taken to a metal-stone slab where thirteen women stabbed me in the back. Peggy was one of them. Through my piss-stained eyeballs I was able to recognize a few of the others. There was Barbara Niederman, a woman whose husband I'd once worked for. As she stabbed me, I could smell the sweat from the soles of her feet. I felt toes in my mouth but then the toes turned into the worst parts of a squid.

My face was in Joe's ass, my mouth sucking on a slimy new appendage. The greasy, whitish substance was running down my chin. Then Pam the waitress stabbed me right under my neck and my scrotum tingled. Joe fell over.

Peggy had hit him in the side of the head with a solid piece of old clay. Joe's face contorted in surprise and he was on the ground. His stovepipe hat was off and I nearly choked when I saw what it had been covering.

Chunks of his skull were missing and in their place were pulsating squid parts, squeezing back and forth through the holes and around his brain. Grey and white slop oozed from Joe's skull and he mumbled a few words as he convulsed, grabbing handfuls of clay.

"Jim," Peggy said, probably not knowing what to say. I couldn't blame her. I didn't know what to say either.

I wiped my mouth on my shirtsleeve and stood up. I grabbed Peggy's arm and started walking away. We could hear wet slurping sounds coming from every hole in Joe's body. I stopped in mid-step and like Lot's wife, I turned back to look at the destruction. However, instead of seeing a society of sex fiends turn to a pile of God-damned rubble, I saw my old friend Joe loudly turning into a shivering mass of human-squid meat.

It dawned on me that Joe was most likely not going to recover from whatever was happening to him. Though I would never usually admit such a thing, my heart ached at permanently losing such a good friend. Joe was one of the only people who stood by me during my turbulent marriage and subsequent divorce. I had to do something.

I wasn't going to stand by and be a spectator to Joe's torment. I let go of Peggy's arm and ran over to him. He was gargling with white, chunky bile and it overflowed over the sides of his face. A burning, fishy smell made my eyes water. Still, I got close enough so that I could grab another hardened piece of clay and then I pummeled my friend's skull until he stopped moving.

Out of his shattered head came mangled pieces of squid and brain. Parts of them were moving, sliding across the clay on white slime.

I was choked up over seeing what had happened to Joe. His yellowed eyeballs sat like chipped marbles attached to licorice. I touched them softly and then walked back over to Peggy.

Apparently, she had been screaming and pleading for me to stop pounding Joe in the head but I hadn't heard her. I don't know if my brain blocked it out or if my ears just decided to stop working during those few moments of mercy that I had given to my friend. Either way, I wouldn't have stopped anyway.

I ran across the clay pits so fast that I was practically lifting Peggy off her feet as I dragged her by her left hand. Her jaw chattered so loudly I was expecting her to leave a trail of broken teeth. I looked back but saw only bits of something twinkling in the moonlight. I thought it might be piss. Maybe Peggy was losing control of her bladder as we sprinted.

It was a strange sensation: running in one direction while looking in another. I was experiencing a strange weightlessness, wind forcing itself into my ear and nose and my legs feeling like confused spider-appendages trying to construct themselves into geometric puzzles.

Peggy's face turned pale, her high cheekbones splintering off into triangles of bone. Her round face became a gravestone balloon complete with a large nose that bore the inscription: *If I had done this a long time ago, it would have saved a lot of pain.*

Saved it for what? I thought to myself. Or saved it from whom? I was in no condition to try to come up with any answers. I was too busy trying to gain some sort of ground beneath my feet. I was having no such luck. My legs felt like they were being manipulated against my will, as if my brain was apathetic to my physical movements.

I kept my eyes on Peggy's stone face.

My own face was tingling and I smelt the warm, wet stench of Joe's brain as well as the underside of Barbara Niederman's feet. I tasted toes and I tasted squid. I tasted the burning fluid from an old jelly jar. The enamel of my teeth flaked off into snowflakes that bombarded automobiles made out of bone. Primitive men and women opened their mouths and swallowed the tooth-snow, swallowing the pieces until my teeth rested in their bellies and I ached to move through their colons and out into the world again.

Peggy's round stone face darkened and she started complaining about the size of her nose and the blisters on her feet. A laugh escaped the right side of my mouth.

And that's when we hit the deer.

PART TWO
The Synchronicity of Shining Squid

"I am now the most miserable man living. If what I feel were equally distributed to the whole human family, there would not be one cheerful face on the earth. Whether I shall ever be better I cannot tell; I awfully forebode I shall not. To remain as I am is impossible…"

Abraham Lincoln

"I don't know why you are treating me like this. The only thing I have done is carry a pistol into a movie."

Lee Harvey Oswald

CHAPTER TEN
Black Boned Keith

Keith limped down Price Street.

He had blisters on his feet from the walk but he was proud of himself for not taking too many breaks. He spotted the house, walked up to the front steps and stopped.

Nice house, Keith thought, *Very comfy*. He thought that he would like to have a house just like it someday. It was small but quant and resembled a gingerbread house with an odd triangular design. *It was a house out of a fantasy*, Keith realized. *It was someone's dream house*.

The street was silent for a few minutes and then Keith heard the pulsating hum of a factory in the distance. Once he heard the sound, he couldn't escape it. It was like the heartbeat of the town, underneath all of the roaring engines of automobiles, frantic babbling of housewives and aggravated murmurings of their husbands. That hum was the foundation that held the gyrating vibration of television signals and radio frequencies.

Without this hum, the town would be a fucking ghost, Keith thought. He wondered if the people who lived in the town still heard the sound throughout the day or if their minds and ears just blocked it out. When the townspeople fucked, did they grind their hips to the factory-hum in lieu of sexy music on the radio? Did they cum aloud to the low industrial roar in the distance?

Keith bent down and plucked a piece of crabgrass from the lawn. He rolled it between his fingers and put it to his mouth as it were a yellow-brown cigarette. He did this almost unconsciously and continued to attempt to puff on it, half-expecting smoke to force its way out of the blade of grass. Standing up, Keith spit the grass out of his mouth and walked up to the door, almost tripping over three days worth of newspapers.

One of the headlines caught Keith's eye: *The Deed Done at Ford's Theatre Last Night.* He shivered at the implications. What deed? It sounded ominous to Keith as if the headline was really a coded message to a fellow conspirator. Though the words piqued his curiosity, Keith didn't pick up the paper. He knew that if he did, he would be too distracted from the task at hand.

His arms and legs felt like lead pipes. Keith lifted his left leg and found that it took more effort than usual. He did the same with is left arm and then his right. They were both dead weight. It took Keith much effort to lift his fist up to the door and knock but he managed it. As his knuckles hit the door, he realized that it wasn't made of wood or any other typical construction material but rather it had the color and texture of a crab-shell. It took a second for Keith to realize that it smelled like one, too. The fishy smell made his mouth water. He wanted a drink.

Keith knocked on the door again, his knuckles rubbing against the rough shell. He sucked on his knuckles, trying to soak in the crab taste but only getting dirt and skin. Not hearing a response to his knock, he leaned forward and licked the door.

The tiny bumps of the shell tore up his tongue and excreted small drops of liquid that mixed with Keith's blood. More drops collected at the base of his mouth. He swallowed and felt the heaviness from his arms and legs disappear. He continued to lick the door.

Then he found himself in the street watching as a man slobbered all over a door. The man's arms floated up as if filled with helium. He resembled a marionette attached to the door by his face, arms and legs moving up and down as they tried to escape the body.

Keith walked to the curb, still watching the man at the door. *Nice house*, he thought to himself. *It was someone's dream house.* He sensed, not so much with his eyes as with his mind, ethereal strings attached to the marionette-man. His tongue got rawer with each lick. The marionette knocked again and put his ear to the door.

Keith listened but again did not hear anything from inside the house. He tried the doorknob. It turned all the way and clicked. Keith pushed the door open and brushed up against the crab shell one last time.

As he entered, his eyes scanned the house but he realized that his mind wasn't actually taking anything in. His thoughts were in the forefront of his head and therefore created a shield in front of his vision. He saw what was expected but in a hazy representation of solid matter.

The room was a musty but tidy hologram, brownish-yellow and silent. Keith felt his bowels ache from the suspense. He put his fingers to the wall and forced his eyes to concentrate on the stale paint. In the uneven textures and drips, he saw the kitchen and smelled its dull linoleum. The whiff of cheap cigars, spilt whisky and peanuts made his nostrils open and close like fish gills.

In a long bubble of paint, Keith saw a vision of the upstairs bedroom but more specifically, he saw the knife mark in the wooden headboard of the bed. He rubbed his index finger along it and dug his fingernail into it, hoping to make another mark on the headboard. Instead, he tore open a pillow, spilling polyester foam across the yellow sheets.

"Who the hell are you? Get out!" a voice shouted from behind Keith. He took his hand off the wall and turned his head. A gray-haired man stood behind him wearing stained black denim pants and a brown-stained shirt proclaiming that "Millie's Bar-B-Que" on Route 34 had the best ribs in Jersey.

"Red Henry?" Keith asked over his shoulder. He smelt his fingers and got the essence of paint and sweaty high-heels.

"Who the hell are you?" Red Henry shouted. He charged Keith, knocking him nose-first into the wall. Blood splatters appeared on the paint in the shape of an anorexic squid. Henry dug his fingertips into Keith's side, his hand digging under the ribs like a spoon in a cantaloupe.

Keith smiled and turned his body around, trying to shake Henry loose. As his ribcage was experiencing a phantom penetration, he felt a cotton swab enter his urethra like a prospector. Instead of gold, however, the swab was looking for any sign of pussy and prick disease.

Years ago, Keith had been oblivious to the possibility of sexual diseases until his older brother picked up *Granuloma inguinale* from a prostitute during the war. After hearing all about the wet discomfort of the disease as well as smelling the yellow-green discharge his brother had left on the toilet seat, Keith had gone to a clinic and got tested.

He had entered the room not sure what to expect but not caring that much. The doctor told him to take his pants off and then immediately grabbed Keith's penis. Out of nowhere, a long cotton swab appeared and was forced into Keith's unsuspecting urethra. Before he knew it, the process was over and Keith stood shocked, stunned and numb. It didn't hurt but it was an unexpected penetration that made him feel like a rape victim. Even so, Keith became obsessed with the sensation and indulged in small rape fantasies of his own, using matchsticks, coffee stirrers, the skinny end of pen-caps, broken prongs of plastic forks, and any other object that piqued his arousal.

Red Henry slammed Keith's head into the wall again as they struggled. The back of his skull dented the sheetrock causing bloodstained dust to spurt into a red-white cloud in one silent poof. Keith lost his balance and fell against the wall, his ass hitting the hardwood floor like a hammer.

Two hands grabbed Keith and turned him over. Red Henry put a knee into his back and took a long, thin root out of his pocket. He wrapped it around Keith's neck and pulled.

"Know what this is? It's my lucky shoestring." Red Henry tightened the root, loosened it, and then tightened it again. "Got it from my friend John De Conker." Keith's hands grabbed at his neck.

"Now, who are you and what the hell are you doing in my house?" he said, loosening the root around Keith's neck again. His eyes glazed over and his mind moved on to other things. "You come here looking for Mr. Timothy? He's not here, goddamn it," he said, his hands twitching and weakening. "Is that why you're here? Tell that Blue Christ fellow to leave me alone!"

Keith sensed the weakness in Henry's hands and took advantage of it. He turned over and grabbed the root from Red Henry's hands. With the root no longer strangling him, Kevin spat a glob of drool onto the floor. It fell into the disemboweled shape of a Japanese spider crab. Keith let his forehead fall into the crab's innards. In its stomach, he discovered the mangled flesh of a drowned man and the remains of a stovepipe hat.

Red Henry landed a punch in Keith's side and then ran out of the room. The punch shook Keith and a tiny bit of vomit slid up his throat and into his mouth. He let it drip onto the crab and it formed the tentacles of a squid that wrapped around the remains.

A door slammed and Keith heard footsteps trotting down stairs. He got up and walked to the kitchen. Rummaging through drawers, he pocketed three old matchbooks, some pennies, and a used chopstick. He then left through the backdoor.

"Laura didn't warn me about this shit," he said, walking out through the yard and onto the sidewalk. He lit a cigarette. "Sorry, Smitty," he said. "But I really need a smoke right now." Walking down Price Street, he turned onto Jefferson Road and took the root from his pocket.

I'm in the mood for pancakes, Keith thought and then proceeded to stick the thin end of the root into his left nostril.

CHAPTER ELEVEN
Jim

The deer was dead already, probably shot for fun by a kid or a drunken hunter. It looked like another animal had gotten to it as well. My feet fell into the mess and I dragged Peggy down onto the ground, our surroundings becoming a swirl of dark green and grey. I landed a foot or two in front of the deer by Peggy fell on the animal. She laid there up to her elbows in deer guts. I turned over and looked up at the moon.

No longer was there a man in the moon. There was a squid showing me a tentacled apocalypse squirming and inking across the sky until its sigil was tattooed in every cell of every brain of every human being.

My head started to hurt. I closed my eyes hoping that it would decrease the pain of the migraine-assassination. I shook my head and it rattled, a half-inch bullet from a derringer pistol sliding its way through in search of my pineal gland.

I tasted old paint and blood. My teeth and tongue moved the grit around into my cheeks and then I swallowed. I heard Peggy sloshing around in the blood, trying to get up.

"Don't move….just wait," I whispered.

"Fuck you," Peggy replied. Her voice was smooth and sweet like cheap milk chocolate.

"My back hurts," I said even though that wasn't really the reason why I told her not to move. My back and its scars always hurt. However, I knew that even if she were in an extremely sympathetic mood, it wouldn't persuade her to stay in the deer gore any longer than she had to.

Despite the pain, I helped Peggy off her feet. I started to wonder where she got the matching gloves and boots. Were we going to a party? Was it Halloween? No, of course not. There were no gloves. Her hands and feet were slick with deer blood.

We started walking again but this time I kept my eyes looking straight ahead, on the lookout for deer and other potential obstacles. I figured we had about a mile to walk but I wasn't sure. I was always bad with estimating distances.

Peggy shook her arms, flicking blood on the back of my neck. I expected it to be warm but it felt as if it had no temperature at all. Her feet were drenched in red too and I thought that if it had been covered in something other than deer blood, I would have licked them clean. Chocolate sauce, maybe, or caramel. I'd prefer something that wasn't too sweet and wouldn't interfere with the natural taste of her feet.

We walked as fast as we could manage. There was no conversation as Peggy was intent on scraping the now-dried blood off her body. I thought back to how we ended up here and how I had met Peggy.

It was right after I had quit running shine from the Pine Barrens up to Central Jersey. That's how I had met Joe. I got involved in running his special brand of moonshine down south where the new customers drank it up like water. When I finally decided to quit, I got work full time as a janitor in a department store. It wasn't glamorous but it was something steady and legal.

One day I was called to clean up a spill in the dressing room. It was demeaning work but at that point during the day, my mind was in a forest somewhere, cuddled against a tree. I was beneath a blanket of leaves while I brought the mop over to the mess. As I got close to it, I recognized the scent: urine.

I started mopping it up when someone walked into the booth. It was a cute, skinny blond in a beige skirt. I noticed her legs first: two tan matchsticks ending in three-inch heels.

"Oh, I'm sorry, I was just in here. I left to get another size," she said, straight-faced and holding a pair of pants. I noticed that the bottom of her short skirt was damp.

"I'll be done in a second," I said, not wanting to start a conversation. If there's one thing I had learned working in a department store it is not to start conversations. They either talk your ear off or think you're a pervert. Either way, you lose.

There was a urine puddle in the dressing room she had just used and her skirt was damp. She must have noticed that I was connecting the dots because she smiled and flashed me an intense look.

"Enjoying that?" she asked, nodding her head towards the urine.

"Why would I be?"

"Oh, I don't know," she cooed, coming inside the room and shutting the door. She held up the damp part of her skirt and looked at me, waiting.

"I, uh, don't really know…uh…" I stuttered, looking to the doorknob, wanting to bolt out of there. As much as the situation was intriguing, I didn't want to get fired over a horny housewife and her puddle of piss.

So I did what I thought would cause me the least amount of trouble: I blushed, smiled and walked past her. Carrying my dripping mop away, I left her giggling as she shut the door. I spent the next fifteen minutes in the maintenance room, hoping that by the time I went back, the dressing room would be empty or at least free of the woman with the loose bladder.

The room was empty when I got back but the puddle was back. I shook my head and got to work.

A few days later, the same thing happened but this time the woman lingered around while I cleaned the mess. As I mopped up the last of the mess, she finally introduced herself.

"I'm Lillian, by the way."

"Um, yeah, I'm Jim," I replied, realizing that she probably didn't care what my name was. She was wearing another skirt which was damp with what I presumed to be her fresh urine. The smell lingered with her perfume and wasn't unpleasant at all.

"Well, hello *Jim*. Sorry about that mess. Sometimes I just can't control myself, you know? But you don't mind, do you?" she said, her hands on her hips.

That intimate yet embarrassing meeting jumpstarted a very passionate relationship with Lillian who, after two or three sessions of lovemaking, told me that she preferred to be called by her stage name, Peggy.

"I'm an actress," she told me, "I'm going to be a fucking star. I'm going to be larger than life!"

Her rambling confidence only convinced me that she had some casting-couch connections. I wondered: somewhere in Hollywoodland, was there a high-profile producer with a golden shower fetish? If so, Peggy's shot at stardom was a sure thing.

I wasn't spending my time with her because I was interested in her career choice. In fact, I found it quite embarrassing. Too many aspiring actresses have tap-danced their way in and out of my life and all that was left was an impression of idealistic hopelessness. In other words, they would live and die as pathetic dreamers.

Despite all that, she intrigued me. She was a risk taker, a woman who didn't mind pissing on the floor for a thrill and then embarrassing a scruffy young janitor. I didn't necessarily like to be embarrassed, of course, but it made me slightly excited. Okay, more than slightly.

Peggy and I did things together that I never could have imagined two people doing. I consider myself to be a little bit imaginative, but even in my own late night, lonely-in-bed fantasies I could have never imagined the things we had done.

Trekking through the working class streets of Fisherville felt like a walk on the moon. Every step I took was lopsided. The streetlamps draped an orange hue over everything as we concentrated on walking steadily over uneven sidewalks and curbs.

The factory hummed in the distance and brought back memories both good and bad. Years ago, when I first noticed the sound that reverberated through the town, I imagined it being caused by three huge iron and bronze monks, their humming being a tool to free their minds of whatever earthly garbage it may contain. In a way, that hum cleared my mind, too.

We walked past the Knights of Columbus building and its neon-lit miniature Virgin Mary enclosed in smudged glass. The back of my head tingled as I remembered kneeling in front of it years ago, waiting for an answer to my problems. I never received one.

Peggy's hand made its way to my back and her fingers traced my scar. She poked it with her fingernail.

"Christ, Peggy, watch it!"

"So sorry, love, I forgot," she purred, moving her hand away. I pointed to a street sign three blocks away.

"We're almost there."

"Thank god."

"This has been one hell of a fucking night," I said, realizing that it was an understatement like no other.

"It can only get better," Peggy said, sucking out some remnants of deer blood from underneath her fingernails.

CHAPTER TWELVE
Black Boned Keith

Pancakes were still on his mind when Keith spotted Jim and Peggy walking hand in hand in the moonlight.

A sharp smile split his face open to reveal Keith's very yellow but very straight teeth. Red Henry's root was in his left hand and a Pall Mall was in his right. He dropped the cigarette and slipped the root back into his jacket pocket. The smile disappeared as the pain in his knee intensified. It started to click with each step.

Keith was annoyed. He had arrived at Red Henry's house too early. Laura had wanted him at the house *after* Jim but the car accidents had made sure that her plans were ruined. Keith wasn't annoyed because he cared about Laura's plans. She had her reasons for asking him this favor but they didn't concern him. Instead, Keith was pissed because, in a way, Jim had gotten the better of him, as did Red Henry.

"My father's harmless," Laura had told Keith.

"But if he tries to stop me?"

"Push him aside or something but you're going to have to end up making it look like Jim did it and that means using a knife."

"What about Peggy?"

"She knows what to do."

"I hope so," Keith muttered, watching Jim and Peggy walk toward him, towards Price Street. He quickly planned a route in his mind and started to run down a side street in order to come up to the backside of Red Henry's place.

On Douglas Street, Keith saw the back of the house. He'd have to cut through someone's side yard but he wasn't too concerned. The house was quiet and dark with no signs that a dog was present.

Hopping the fence in one quick motion, Keith walked over crabgrass to the back fence. He made his way over, reached the back corner of Red Henry's house, and waited.

A few minutes passed. Slightly heavy breathing and footsteps echoed up Price Street. After Keith heard the front door open and close, he walked up the left side of the house and up the front steps.

Keith caressed the crab-shell and opened the door. He was greeted by a warm fist that rattled the teeth from his gums.

CHAPTER THIRTEEN
Jim

"Next time you sneak up on someone, try not to make so much fucking noise," I said to Keith while he was on the floor, holding his bloody mouth. I have to confess that it wasn't just his squeaky shoes that gave him away. The soft night wind brought the smell of cigarettes to my nose and I saw a shadow on the side of Red Henry's house.

I figured someone was waiting for me and after the events of the evening, I wasn't too surprised. As I was mentally patting myself on the back, I heard someone stomping up the basement steps. Red Henry flew through the door.

"Jimmy!" Red Henry shouted. He put his hand out but then thought better of it. Instead, he put his arms around me. "C'mere, son." He hugged me hard and I wondered if he even noticed Keith picking up his own teeth from the floor.

"Henry, how you feeling? Laura called me, she thought something was wrong." I returned the hug.

"Oh, I'm fine except that this asshole right here broke into my house and stole my root." Red Henry had noticed Keith after all.

"Root? What root? What are you talking about? This guy was here before?" I asked, giving Keith a kick in the ribs. Peggy gasped as if she thought I should go easy on him.

"My lucky root, my devil's shoestring, the one I got in Louisiana when I met Laura's mother. This little son of a bitch stole it!" Red Henry nearly spit on Keith's head.

I grabbed the collar of Keith's jacket and stuck my fingers into his bleeding mouth, shoving them around like an epileptic dentist. His eyes filled with tears. "You bite me, you're dead," I told him. "What the fuck are you doing here, Keith?" The last time I had seen Keith was when he had asked for a piece of the moonshine action. I had declined and he had not been pleased. The guy thought that just because I cooked his pancakes every week, he was entitled to become my business partner.

He obviously couldn't speak while my hand was in his mouth so I took it out and let him catch his breath. His voice sounded like a squid's voice if a squid could talk after years of smoking a pack a day.

"Downstairs," he said, "money."

Of course. What other fucking reason does anyone have for breaking into a house?

Keith was losing a lot of blood, so much so that I was wondering if he had already been bleeding on the way in. There was a platter of blood in front of him. In the middle of it were a couple of yellowish teeth. Keith's eyes didn't look right.

"Dead babies," he said. He was delirious, yes, but he reminded me of the satchels in Fred's car and the one that I had left in the woods. He kept talking through a broken mouth: words strewn together by a fading consciousness.

I said, "What the hell do you know about the dead babies?"

"You fuckin' Christ don't know shit need smoke smitty fuckin' taxi shit," Keith replied.

I turned around and saw Peggy sitting with her arms wrapped around herself, scared and confused.

I looked at Red Henry. "Is there money downstairs?"

"What? Money? No, no, I don't keep my money downstairs. I don't even have any money, shit. I gave my savings to Laura's little sister. She's having a hard time, you know. Her husband has some problems, sold a lot of the stuff in the house for dope. Even stole from me the last time they were here."

"Then what's downstairs?" I asked.

"Oh, downstairs, downstairs, yeah, that's right. Yeah, you got it. Downstairs, Jimmy, downstairs. I'm going to need my root back," he said. That familiar glaze came over his eyes. He started rummaging through Keith's pockets and found his root.

Keith grabbed my ankle and pulled it forward. I fell right on the boney part of my ass. It hurt like hell. I shoved my foot into his face, landing on his nose causing a cracking sound that made Peggy gasp yet again.

The floor was slippery so my first attempt off the floor was shaky but I managed it. Red Henry was staring at the wall and twisting the root around in his hands. He started heading for the cellar.

There was a soft knock on the front door. I figured it had to be Laura. I opened it slowly, my hands ready just in case. I relaxed as I saw the pretty face and figure of my ex-wife.

"Laura, this is a fucking mess," I said, motioning for her to look at Keith on the ground. Her eyes lit up in surprise.

"Oh my god, what happened?" she asked, putting her hand on my shoulder. I looked over at Peggy to see if she had noticed.

"This guy broke into your dad's house before and then came back after we showed up," I said.

"Oh my god….I told you someone was there when I talked to him on the phone! Leaving someone his age here is dangerous especially someone with his condition," she said, reminding me of our fight concerning Red Henry's potential move into our house. She had needed her space. She hadn't wanted the burden of her father. I, on the other hand, wouldn't have minded taking care of him.

"We should have taken him in," I said. Her eyes turned to narrow slits.

"Oh, don't give me that shit. You think we had the money for that? Do you think I have the money for that now? Maybe you should be telling this to Gina, my dad's little princess," she said. I was then reminded of why we had divorced in the first place. Despite her obvious intellectual prowess, Laura was a cold and bitter person. Any act of kindness or sweetness she showed was only done after precise calculation of how it would benefit her.

"You're still a goddamn bitch, Laura," I said. I hadn't wanted to say it, not really. I wanted her to know it, sure, but saying it would have let her know that I was harboring a grudge and that meant she still had some power over me.

"And you're still a fucking drunk, still a naïve son of a bitch that'll trust anyone who gives him attention," she said, her mouth twisted showing off more wrinkles than I realized she had. Her eyes darted to Peggy.

Keith poked his head up and looked around. He looked at Laura and said, "Sorry I fucked it up."

CHAPTER FOURTEEN
Black Boned Keith

Laura shook her head and started to turn around. Keith's head dropped and hit the wooden floor with a thump. Jim's eyes widened. He looked at the two of them in cold disbelief.

"What the fuck is he talking about, Laura?" Jim asked.

"Nothing, Jim. Nothing at all."

"Fucking bitch!" Jim grabbed Laura's arm.

"Don't touch me!" Laura hissed. Jim let go and looked down at Keith who was now shivering with a handful of teeth. They rattled like dice.

Jim backed up, grabbed Peggy's hand, and led her to the cellar. The door was unlocked. They started down slowly. With each creak of the stairs, Peggy's hand loosened from Jim's grip.

The basement was dry and cold. Old Fisherville bricks made up the walls as they did in most of the houses that were built in the town within the first hundred years of its founding. In the years prior to the War, it was the world's largest manufacturer of bricks. Fisherville's clay was perfect for brick making and when the demand was high, the town became a haven for those looking for work: mostly immigrants and men trying to escape a past that was dull, domesticated, or criminal.

Jim eyes darted from one stylized letter-F to another. When he reached the bottom of the stairs, Peggy was no longer holding his hand. The room was empty except for rusty buckets, milk crates, and cardboard boxes. Jim heard rattling from the small room off the far corner of the basement.

Jim looked into the small room. Red Henry stood holding a jar under a light bulb. Shelves covered the walls. The shelves held other large, cloudy jars of moonshine.

In each jar, there floated an infant.

Red Henry turned around to face Jim. He held up the jar. The infant inside shimmered and reminded Jim of a carnival sideshow attraction. Except this attraction was one that someone was going to drink.

"They moved me, Jimmy and now I know my purpose," Red Henry said, his eyes glazed over.

CHAPTER FIFTEEN
Jim

When I saw Red Henry holding the jar, I squinted and let my jaw fall open. I saw Fred and his satchels projected on a wobbly movie screen in my mind along with the satchel I left in the woods. Joe Gurney assaulting Peggy with a squid wrapped around his brain. His liquid seafood shit was still crusted on my lips and beard. Fred was dead in the trunk of his car, his eye socket resembling fruit compote. Keith frequenting the restaurant I had worked at and eventually he made a proposition that we should work together running shine.

This whole thing was like some huge torturous puzzle where none of the pieces should fit but they do anyway. It was like a big joke being played on me. That paranoid side of me was right. Everyone was out to get me. Everyone had a secret they were keeping from me.

Looking at Red Henry and his room, I was disgusted but surprisingly in the mood for pancakes.

I looked at Red Henry in disbelief. "Jesus Christ, what did you do?"

CHAPTER SIXTEEN
Black Boned Keith

"Jesus Christ, what did you do?" Jim said. He was interrupted by a six-inch blade to the back. Peggy stuck it in as if she was carving out a melon. There was a small smile of delight on her face. Laura stared coldly with her arms folded. Keith had dragged himself down the stairs and was on the cement floor, watching in disbelief as he saw that whore Peggy shove a knife into Jim's back.

To Keith, it looked as if Jim was taking the stabs in a rhythm, his back bucking forward with every thrust. Blood spurt out in spirals down Jim's back and splattered onto the floor. The way Peggy was moving her arm, Keith was sure that Jim was dead. Her arm shook as if only that part of her was epileptic and her wrist turned so much it looked like it twisted all the way around.

As Peggy made her last stab, Laura walked over to her father. Jim collapsed to the floor and landed on one arm. The other arm swung around to trip Peggy. She fell backwards, her hand still holding the blade. Jim leaned back, slammed his fist on Peggy's wrist so hard that it made a loud crunching sound. Her fingers let go of the knife and Jim's trembling hand grabbed it. He made one slashing motion and Peggy's neck burst, giving birth to a watery, red flower.

"Shit," Keith muttered. He brought himself to his knees and then to his feet.

Laura came out of the corner room, cursed, and rushed over to Jim. They fought over the knife and in the fracas Laura's chest was slashed open. Now under her torn shirt waved a loose flap of skin between her heavy breasts. A deep red hole showed under the flap. Keith looked at it and thought about strawberry compote and pancakes.

Jim let out a groan and sliced Laura one more time. Her hands came up to where her nose used to be. The tip of it was now resting in Jim's beard. Laura fell back onto her ass giving Jim a chance to scoot away. The puddle of blood beneath him allowed for faster movement but Keith was right above him, his foot aimed at Jim's face.

Keith hesitated and Jim noticed. He grabbed the foot and pulled it forward. He shoved the knife into Keith's calf. Between that and his mouth full of blood and teeth fragments, Keith passed out.

Red Henry, meanwhile, was taste testing some of his shine. He choked and pulled out a few strands of hair from his throat. They came out wet and he stuck them onto the brick wall.

With the wounds in his back gushing, Jim crawled over to Henry.

"Henry…help…" he whispered. He was surprised he even managed to make any sound as he felt as if his body was on fire with the core of the inferno resting deep in his back. Though he asked for help, he was fully satisfied to lie down and die on the cold cement floor.

He looked down at the dust and at the stains that covered the floor of the basement. Jim didn't notice it before but all of the dark brown and black stains resembled sea creatures: sharks, squid, octopi, and eels. There were even a few tiny scuffs that looked like humans in the grip or mouth of the creatures. With a rising cacophony of basement-sea sounds, they all began to move, flowing along the surface of the floor. Jim did a backwards crab-walk on all fours toward the wall. His head banged against brick and he slid down, his hair and scalp grinding against the wall. The sound of that grinding reverberated through his skull adding a thunderstorm to the sea sounds.

When Jim whispered, Red Henry turned around, still holding the bottle. He held it up and looked at Jim through the underarm of the floating infant. The moonshine made Jim look pale and ethereal.

"You look like an angel," Red Henry said.

CHAPTER SEVENTEEN
Jim

Everything fucking hurt.

That traitorous bitch Peggy really did a number on my back but the pain had spread throughout my whole body as if my nerve endings decided to have a pain party just for fun. I'm not sure how I managed to fight back.

I could still hear the blood bubbling out of Peggy and Laura was in the corner, crying. Crying over what, I don't know. Maybe she felt bad about the whole thing but my money's on her regretting bring Keith and Peggy in on her plans. Or maybe she was simply crying from the pain. She had a hell of a wound in her chest. Anyway, I didn't really care. If I had enough energy, I would have walked over there and slit her fucking throat, too.

Considering Red Henry's condition and the fact that he was mixed up with the dead infants, I didn't expect him to help me but I pleaded to him nonetheless. Maybe the part of him that I used to know was still in there somewhere or so I hoped.

I was staring at Henry through a jar of moonshine.

And then that psycho pervert Fred appeared, sitting beside me, telling me about the recipe. His deep red eye socket winked at me but it could have been an involuntary spasm. I was again in the mood for pancakes but I ignored the desire. Fred spoke in a lazy voice.

"You know how many people would sell their kids for some scratch? A lot, lemme tell you, Jim. And not just hookers and junkies, either, I'm talking just plain old women who just ain't got that mothering instinct in them. So we buy 'em and sometimes steal them and we do ourselves some business. You know it's all just business, Jim, you know that. It's all for that scratch we gotta itch."

Fred was speaking so close to my left ear that I could feel cold flakes of his spit. The droplets were collecting in my ear and mixing with the earwax. My ear started to burn. I slapped it as if it were simply a fire I could extinguish.

I kept slapping it while Fred talked. He told me about his apartment in South River and about his ex-wife who was also his second cousin. She was the one who introduced him to the pleasures of his favorite type of moonshine. When he started going into great detail about her squid-shaped that smelt like vagina, I sent my knuckles towards his mouth. I hit something cold and sloppy wet. I turned my head to look.

Fred's voice was coming out of a man-sized squid. It was trembling like a freezing child. Right behind it, Peggy was standing up, rubbing a long, moist scar on her neck. She looked at me.

"There goes my fucking film career." Her voice was raspy and a little bit sexy, too. She fell backwards into a pile of basement debris and a puff of dust floated up. It was like something out of one of those slapstick films they show down at the theatre on Main Street. I would have chuckled if I didn't think it'd bring more pain. But deep down I could tell that Peggy was all right. As she lay there, I got the feeling that she was faking it, as if the cut on her throat wasn't as bad as it looked.

I turned to the squid again. The bottom of its head opened up and a beard started to sprout. The beard resembled thousands of wet spider legs, curling in infinite combinations of twists and turns. I was looking through a hairy kaleidoscope and the fucking thing didn't shut up.

"'I have too great a soul to die like a criminal.' You know who said that, Jim?"

"Yeah, I think I do."

"You're smarter than you look, there Jimmy. So who said it?"

"John Wilkes Booth."

"Well, I'll be a sonovabitch!" The Fred-squid trembled and the beard got longer. I have to admit it was making me sick but I was in so much pain I didn't really have a choice but to sit there and become half-hypnotized by the swirling hairy patterns. I saw ragged soldiers in there, marching and drinking, vomiting and shitting. Psychedelic spider-legs turned into half-rusted rifles and crusty-red daggers.

My muscles tightened, relaxed, and then tightened again. I was able to look into my ex-wife's chest cavity from where I sat. I'm sure I don't have to tell you that it wasn't a pretty sight but I couldn't help but feel some sort of relief as if my wasted years with Laura were finally avenged. Her control over me was gone. She sobbed one more time as her chest wound did her in and then she expired like a bad chunk of cheese.

Sic semper tyrannis.

CHAPTER EIGHTEEN
Black Boned Keith / General Entwistle

Keith lost and regained consciousness every few seconds. He watched as pulsating figures in sepia tones were marching to some distant war. Most of these figures had beards like Abraham Lincoln and some were even wearing hats like him, too. Some held knives, some held guns but all held a bottle marked "XXX" in messy white paint. They sang in deep tones while drum and fife music floated in and out of aural focus.

The screen blurred and pale bricks appear along with a bearded man-squid explaining with passionate intensity why it chewed on infant flesh. There was a man next to the squid who was bleeding dark blood from his back. He, too, had a beard but unlike the squid and soldiers, he also possessed a mustache: a spit and shit stained clump of whiskers. The man's tongue flipped out of his mouth like a snake and he rolled his eyes at the squid.

Keith recognized the man next to the squid as Jim Steam, the bootlegger, the moonshine man, the one he was hired to set-up.

As he tried to move, Keith's eyelids fluttered violently.

The scene was on again: scruffy soldiers are half-marching towards some unseen battlefield. Barns and farmhouses are scattered across the landscape. A few cows, sick and milkless, are dotted around the fields. One of the soldiers trembles and falls to the ground, keeping his eyes on one of the animals. Another man walks over, his skin bubbling, causing short blips of memories to fall into Keith's field of thought. The soldier with the bubbling skin speaks.

"James, you alright?"

"I don't know, Bill. I can't..." he replies, trying to stand but failing with a crunch of the kneecap.

"I'll carry you, don't you worry."

Now the other soldiers are tuning into the situation and they gather around James. Some start drinking out of their jugs, turning this small distraction into an excuse to partake in the fog of intoxication.

Keith turned his eyes around in order to get a 360-degree view of the events. Everything was still draped in a brown tint. It reminded him of looking through his grandfather's photo album except in this case there were no naked women, no dead bodies.

A tall but crooked man walks over to James and Bill. It was General Entwistle, a burly bastard who enjoyed deploying his troops into situations that were surely deathtraps. Whenever he watched from a hill as his men were slaughtered, he got an erection that throbbed with every musket fire and cannon blast. He wipes his wet beard with the back of his hand as he puts his other five crusty fingers on Bill's shoulder.

"Now, what would Mr. Lincoln say if he saw you two sons a' bitches stop here like a bunch of pussies? I reckon he wouldn't like it too much, now would he?"

"Sir, this man is hurt, he needs medical attention!"

"Don't raise your voice at me, you fucking cow-humper. What this man needs is a good whack across the crown."

Entwistle swings his jug but misses James' forehead by an inch. Bill almost grabs the general's hand but thinks twice. He puts his hands down at his sides and steps back. He bumps into an extremely drunk private who was taking a gulp out of his vomit-stained jug.

"Pardon me, Junius." Bill mutters. Junius Booth's eyes widen and his mouth opens, revealing a battered set of brown teeth. He puts the jug down and traces the dried vomit shapes with his finger.

"It's all right, my dear Bill. I have a marble head and a marble heart." His voice is sweet, like a child's. He continues to scrape the vomit off the jug until he creates a brown/orange pattern that resembles a squid. Junius' grimy tongue licks it.

Entwistle's squad stop at the sound of Junius' wet tongue as it joins with the vomit-squid. The same feeling floods into each of their minds: the desire to devour something from the sea. At the same time, a gunshot pops and the back of Bill's head weakens in a quick spurt of brains and blood.

"So, the deed is done," Entwistle says, smiling and fingering his erect penis through his pants.

Keith wondered if General Entwistle had anything lodged inside his urethra but quickly dismisses the idea. He considered the general a common thug.

His eyelids fluttered again.

Across the room, Jim stirred and spoke. "Sonovabitch."

Keith crawled over, half of his mind still watching the soldiers while the other half concentrated on picking up Peggy's blade and shoving it deep into Jim's throat.

Jim Steam made one last unsuccessful grasp at Keith and then died, his eyes fixed on the logo of the Fisherville Brick Company.

CHAPTER NINETEEN
General Entwistle

General Entwistle led the rest of his men up toward a barn he suspected was a Confederate hideout.

When they stormed into it, they were not met with the gunfire they had expected but instead walked in on warm silence. Standing amongst jars, body parts, squid parts, and crab legs was a huge, pale man. He was wearing black leather gloves and a stovepipe hat.

General Entwistle was the first to break the silence. "Identify yourself!"

The man looked to his right and to his left. He smiled. "My name is Mr. Timothy." He showed no fear or worry despite being caught committing several illicit and indecent acts. "Can I help you gentlemen?"

"Lord Almighty!" General Entwistle was just starting to get the picture. He may have been a heartless military leader but even he could not help but be disturbed by what he saw. "What have you done?"

Mr. Timothy said, "In simple terms, I'm taking care of business. I'm a business man. However, I must say that I do not think you have any reason to be here. So if you'll excuse me, can you and your men please leave so I may continue my work?" He raised his hands in front of himself, showing off the gore on his black gloves. He dipped a hand into his pocket and pulled out a straight razor. "Boys, if your general here won't lead you out, then please, feel free to partake in some refreshments. Or if you wish, go back to that bastard Lincoln."

Though General Entwistle told his men to stay put, they all listened to Mr. Timothy and grabbed bottles of the vile liquid and drank to their hearts' content. The general's eyes bulged out of his head and finally he raised his gun up to Mr. Timothy. "You dare insult the preserver of the Union? You belong in hell."

"Oh, that is so very poetic. You may rest assured that when I reach hell, your president will be there too, pissing fire in his own tall hat, his skull in a million vile pieces, watching as demonic crabs sodomize his wife." Mr. Timothy smiled. "But I don't have to tell you. You'll see for yourself in time."

A dagger slid across General Entwistle's throat and he fell to his knees before he could get a shot off. Junius Booth dropped the dagger and picked up another jar.

CHAPTER TWENTY
Black Boned Keith

Keith looked down at Jim's dead body. He didn't really feel sorry. Jim had ignored his business proposal and so he got what he had deserved.

His body was a mess and so was his mind. A thousand thoughts spun in a whirlpool at the center of his head. One thing was at the forefront, however, and that was the dead babies in the trunk of that car and in the jars in the basement.

Red Henry was busy drinking the stuff and Keith knew he, in good conscience (at least as much of it as he had left), couldn't let the old man get away with it. Keith had done a lot of shit in his life but he drew the line at dead babies.

With the knife that killed Jim, he hobbled over to Red Henry and stabbed him in the gut. It was a very painful and very slow way to die. Keith picked up a brick and broke Red Henry's ankles. At that moment, he realized, he really did feel in the mood for pancakes.

He managed to get himself upstairs and fell asleep for twelve hours. He dreamt of the fairytale of Puss N' Boots. When he awoke, his thoughts went back to whatever was waiting for him back at his apartment. With a heavy sigh, he left the house.

PART THREE
THERE IS NO SUCH THING AS THE PAST

CHAPTER TWENTY ONE
Black Boned Keith / Smitty

The trip home was difficult but Keith managed to get there in one piece. After all that had happened, the one thing he looked forward to was seeing Smitty. He was still aware of the fact, however, that something else was waiting for him and it was not good.

He ignored the sights and smells of South River and instead set his mind on getting to his apartment safely. He entered the building, walked up the stairs two at a time and got to the top. At the end of the hallway, there stood the same figure that he saw while leaving his apartment the previous day. It was a huge man dressed in a suit and wearing black, leather gloves. A glistening straight razor was in his right hand. He smiled. "Ah, Keith, you're back."

"Who're you?" Keith realized that this was probably the man whose car he crashed into, the one with the babies in the trunk. He felt some fear but not enough to send him running.

The man said, "My name is Mr. Timothy. You don't know me, Keith, but your brother does. We met during the war. He owes me a rather substantial amount of product and I can't seem to locate him." Mr. Timothy's body was flickering as if he wasn't entirely there in the hallway with Keith. "I'll need his whereabouts. If you cannot supply me with that, then I'll settle for your corpse."

Keith's brain twisted and turned through memories: his brother telling him war stories about a guy named Simon Timothy who did terrible things to the wives and children of enemy soldiers. What was the connection between this man and his brother? Keith didn't know. What he did know was that he wasn't going to rat out his brother but he also wasn't going to let himself get killed over it.

"You're not getting either."

"Oh, Keith," Mr. Timothy laughed disappointedly. He squatted down, dropped his pants, and let loose a deluge of feces, wet hair, crab parts, and milk. The mess started to bubble and it all came together, forming a feces-crab with wet, tangled hair on the top of its misshapen head. It opened a mouth-like orifice and let out a scream that sounded like the gongs of a Buddhist monastery.

Keith stood paralyzed.

A door opened in the hallway and out came a man dressed in nothing but a diaper. "Keep the fucking noise down, people!" The man ran up to Mr. Timothy without noticing the creature. With a flick of its claw, the creature took off the man-baby's head sending it flying down the hallway. That's when Keith made a run for his apartment door. When he got there, the door opened on its own and he looked down to see Smitty trembling in fear. The small squid slithered on its juices out into the hallway and attacked the crab-shit creature. It was a blur of tentacles, fishy squid arms, and crab claws. Fluids and flakes of shit splattered the walls and floor of the hallway. Mr. Timothy sat watching the battle.

Then his head exploded.

Keith stood in the doorway holding a shotgun. He put two more rounds into the chamber and pointed it at the creature. "Smitty, get out of there!" The squid didn't move. It was intent on finishing the fight itself.

"Goddamnit, Smitty. Move!" Keith reluctantly put his arms into middle of the fight. Crab claws scraped his skin. Keith watched a version of himself being dissected, the body parts being used along with those of Lincoln and Booth in order to make some sort of mechanized assassin-victim hybrid. It would spend eternity annihilating itself, finding new ways to explode, puncture and penetrate its own body.

Keith shook himself out of it, grabbed Smitty and threw himto safety. He kicked at the crab-shit thing and picked up the shotgun. He quickly aimed and as a claw came up toward him, he fired.

The creature became a trembling mound of mush.

Smitty whimpered and Keith ran toward him. "Are you okay, Smitty?" The small squid let out a high-pitched whistle and then died.

Tears filled Keith's eyes. He would bury the squid that afternoon. Then he'd call his brother and tell him about the visit from Mr. Timothy.

Perhaps after that, he'd take a nice, long nap.

CHAPTER TWENTY TWO
Peggy Entwistle

Peggy applied more make-up to her neck, covering the scar. "That about does it," she said, looking forward to her first official role on the silver screen. She had already talked to the producer, George Archainbaud and he seemed to think that Peggy had talent.

He had said to her, "Peggy darling, you are going to be a big star and I'm going to make it happen! You're going to be working with one the best directors in town. He's a little queer, likes wearing a suit made out of crab shells, but he's a real talent and every film he's made has been a hit."

Peggy had eagerly agreed to meet with the director. She bought a fancy new wardrobe and got her hair done.

Things are really looking up, she thought. *My life is going to be perfect.*

CHAPTER TWENTY THREE
A Month Later: The End

Peggy was drunk. She had lost the film role to someone she knew was less talented. The slut probably gave that smelly bastard Archainbaud a blowjob. On top of that, Peggy's father was giving her grief about her wild lifestyle. He wanted her to settle down, get married, and have children. He wanted her to be more disciplined. But how could she be? She wasn't an army brat like him.

Everything was going against her.

So in order to combat everything that, Peggy climbed up to the top of the big H and made her final impact on Hollywoodland. Before she jumped, she thought about Jim Steam and how she had betrayed him. She almost felt bad but figured that if she hadn't done it, someone else would've. But he had been a pretty good screw and it was a waste to have thrown that away just for some easy cash.

Peggy took one last look at the sky and then jumped.

She splattered on the ground below, the pieces of her body jumbled in a sloppy mess that resembled a tentacled sea creature.

A gang of stray cats came over to survey the damage. They sniffed and meowed like furry investigators. Curious, they got closer and closer. The cats, seeing Peggy's face, scurried like mice. They wanted no part of her.

THE END

APPENDIX I
LINCOLN'S ASSASSIN FACE

Abraham Lincoln woke up covered in dank, green sweat. He had had that dream again, the one where he is shot in the head by that squid with the giant breasts. One minute he's looking at some slippery slimy cleavage, thinking about sticking his flesh-pistol in there and then the next minute, BAM, his brains are splattered all over a theatre balcony.

There was a time in his life when he would have believed the dream to be an omen, a sign warning him of imminent danger. But a hard life had taught him that there was nothing to be gained from dreams except an occasional nocturnal emission. It was odd, though, how much the green sweat resembled the discolored semen that was produced from those periodic emissions. If it wasn't for his growing distrust of doctors, he might have sought some medical attention.

Even so, he was glad the dream was over. He got out of bed, making sure not to disturb his wife since she had become such a light sleeper. She was down to eighty pounds and blind. She was gradually turning into a mole. Lincoln was convinced that it was those goddamn confederates who were behind it. Was nothing sacred to them? It was his *wife*, goddamnit.

On the other hand, weren't moles clever creatures? Perhaps he could train her. Were moles even trainable? He'd have to find out.

Lincoln walked to the corner of the room and looked down into his spittoon to make sure that his birthday cake was still there. It was. It sat there in all its glory: a soft and sugary rectangle covered in gooey phlegm provided by the Chinese prostitutes he had hired. Those yellow whores had given him trouble at first. They didn't want to comply with his wishes despite his paying them a handsome sum.

Eventually they gave in and spat on the cake that he now hovered over. He'd eat it later.

He went downstairs, careful not to disturb his kittens who were busy playing poker. Those bastards were always gambling. And now they had taken up smoking pipes, too. If they weren't so damn cute, he'd kick them out of the house. But if he did that, who would help with his memoirs? God knew that his wife was in no shape to do it. The cats were his only hope in the matter. He still had two volumes to go and he wasn't getting any younger.

Once he was in the kitchen Lincoln made himself some breakfast: two hairy eggs and a glass of donkey milk. He loved the stuff. When he was a boy living in Kentucky, it was practically all he had eaten. His parents had been worried about his diet but he assured them that it was exactly what the Lord wanted him to eat.

So Abraham Lincoln sat in the kitchen, eating his breakfast, thinking about his parents.

He was chewing so loudly that he didn't hear me as I snuck up on him. I put the pistol to his head and then whispered, "This is for Jim, you bastard!" and then BAM-BAM-BAM. A bunch of presidential rice-krispie treats splattered across the kitchen.

His wife ran down the stairs but instead of attacking me, she ran outside and dug into the ground. She had a nice ass for a mole. I'd like to stick my flesh-pistol in there, I thought. Why not?

I walked up to her and said, "Sic semper tyrannis."

She stuck her ass up out of the hole and said, "Where's the beef?"

I stuck my tentacle-manhood inside her, answering her question with a forceful thrust.

She screamed, "God bless America!" while I freed my semen-slaves into the expanse of her gaping mole snatch.

APPENDIX II
A REPORT OF BIOMECHANICAL EXORCISMS
IN THE AMERICAN CIVIL WAR

Fresh meat .. real houses .. warm women .. dreams of my defeated men .. but I do not let them write home .. they can stare at the trees & pretend they're wives .. wood skin covering pale bodies beneath the moss ..

I have to remind them .. just eat the rations, boys .. & watch out for injuns & their fire spit .. it'll turn your brain to flakes of iron mush ..

Oh, the horrors of red liquor hell .. goddamned pagans .. violating virgins .. sleeping with machines .. pumping blood of metals .. scalps & gears pulsating beneath red epidermis .. devil worshippers .. bottles of teeth & whiskey in the barn .. the battle was lost from the beginning .. put your guns down .. it's all just a barrel of iron & viscera .. absurd assassinations .. numerous spiders spy on me through trap doors .. they transform my limbs into tree branches & gun metal .. mesmerizing drunken red gods .. shattering bones into pieces of machine meat .. like john the rotator ..

Lincoln & ghosts in the crimson room .. political advice from mechanized ectoplasm .. sometimes the stars move & perform surgery on me with electromagnetic slime .. nature & organization explode.. my body is nothing more than a crooked & disappointing machine of flesh .. digesting duck parts .. defecating harmonic milk .. maids service the skin-wrapped rod .. electrical performances sparking mental automation & dusty arcs of action .. steam & turbines .. pancakes & axles .. flapjack off the grid .. like john the revelator ..

Oh, the horrors of simple wheels & fleshy leather feet ..
stinking aroma of hydraulic toes tapping along the gears .. cotton
corncob .. cock-skinner creek .. pickpockets with faces made of steel
and envy .. when will we end this war for squid parts .. squid spirits ..
squid shine .. squid gods .. in the morning meshes .. like john de
conker ..

With a heavy heart .. & pen in hand .. I am ordering my men
to retreat .. retreat .. retreat ..

APPENDIX III
ASSASSINATION'S SECRET DOMAIN

Shotgun Man walked into the bar and took a good look at every man's face.

The target, Johnny Balance was supposed to be there between the hours of three and six in the afternoon. It was like some sort of ritual for him and Shotgun Man was going to use that ritual to his advantage.

"Help you?" the bartender said to Shotgun Man.

The bartender's face was covered in deep wrinkles that reminded Shotgun Man of the scars he saw on that prostitute back in Detroit. Her back had been a map of knife wounds and broken beer bottle surgeries. Poor girl would have done anything for a buck.

Shotgun Man said, "Just beer."

The bartender did nothing to hide his impatience. "Jesus Christ, what kind?" Shotgun Man put his hands palm-down on the bar and said, "Just beer."

"Foreign? Domestic? What?"

"Just beer." He stared at the bartender. He didn't blink. He didn't move.

The bartender got the message and the wrinkles in his face flushed with frightened blood. "Sure thing." He grabbed a glass and filled it with beer from the nearest tap. Placing it in front of Shotgun Man, he said, "On the house."

"Thank you." Shotgun Man grabbed the glass of beer but did not drink it. He scanned the room again for Johnny Balance. The man was supposed to be there so why wasn't he?

There were no women in the bar and that felt strange to Shotgun Man. There should be at least one whorish barfly in the place even at three-thirty in the afternoon. He didn't think it was a gay bar but if it was, he wanted to make quick work of Johnny Balance so he could get the hell out of there.

He was looking at a man at the far end of the bar when he smelt something. It wasn't any of the usual smells you'd encounter in a bar. It wasn't alcohol or peanuts. It wasn't piss or belches.

It was pancake batter.

Shotgun Man knew the smell very well. He cooked himself breakfast every morning and it was almost always pancakes. They weren't made from scratch, though. He always bought the pancake powder that just had to be mixed with water. The smell and taste of the batter were unique. It was something that Shotgun Man looked forward to and he often ended up eating half the batter before it was made into pancakes.

He'd always thought that the smell and taste of pancake batter was a combination of raw eggs and semen. Shotgun Man wasn't ashamed to admit that he had smelt his own semen before. However, he was also proud to say that he hadn't tasted it. If he had, though, he guessed it might taste a little bit like pancake batter.

Shotgun Man put his beer down and looked around to see if anyone was in the process of mixing up a batch of pancakes. No one was doing any such thing. However, his behavior was causing several of the men in the bar to stare at him, wondering who the weird guy was who was.

"You smell that?" Shotgun Man said to the bartender.

The bartender was busy scratching the wrinkles in his face. The wrinkles seemed to have multiplied and were now covering his neck. They were also a deep shade of red now. He said, "Smell what?"

"Pancakes."

"Pancakes? What the hell you talking about?"

Shotgun Man tapped his knuckles on the bar. "I said pancakes." He couldn't believe how hard-headed the bartender was being. It wasn't like back in Sicily. Back there, the men who tended to the bar were smart men who knew what to say to their customers especially to someone like Shotgun Man.

"You crazy or something? Get the fuck outta my bar," the bartender said, waving his hand. The fear he had felt earlier had left him only to be replaced by dumb courage.

"No."

"You just get off the boat or something? I'm throwing you out. You don't have a choice. Want me to call the cops?"

"No."

"Jesus Christ!" the bartender said. He threw his hands up and walked away.

Shotgun Man watched as the man made his way to a door in the back of the bar. Was he going to get a weapon? Call the police? Maybe he had a gang of tough guys back there ready to beat the shit out of any stubborn Sicilian who came through the door.

He looked at the other patrons to see if anyone was going to take the bartender's side in the conflict. No one was paying attention anymore. They were all just sipping their beers and watching the ballgame on the small television that was on a shelf in the corner. Shotgun Man thought about baseball and still didn't understand the appeal. It was a slow game but it wasn't slow in the way that chess was slow. There didn't seem to be any real strategy involved in baseball, at least not enough to justify the tedious pace. Seeing the men drink their beer and stare at the television made Shotgun Man uneasy. It was as if they were seeing something he couldn't. Maybe there were secret codes or symbols in the game. Maybe each game was some sort of occult ritual and all those baseball statistics that people memorize were really magick spells.

Shotgun Man eyed up the men in the bar, seeing them now in red and black robes. They had drawn a diamond shape on the floor in chalk and were standing around it, reciting cryptic combinations of letters and numbers. What the hell were they doing?

White dust filled the room, covering the men in a thick blanket. Shotgun Man closed his eyes and held his breath. Was it poison gas? Had Johnny Balance been waiting for him with an army of baseball cultists?

"Son bitches," Shotgun Man said. He pulled his gun out and fired several rounds into the dust cloud. There was the sound of deep groaning and then skin hitting skin. Once the dust cleared, Shotgun Man saw that the cultists were now playfully slapping each other in the face.

"You crazy. All of you," Shotgun Man said. "I come back and then you're all dead." He put his gun away and walked to the door. He took one last look at the men and spat on the ground. As soon as the saliva hit the ground, the men in the bar stopped their activity and stared at Shotgun Man.

"What? Why you looking at me now? You have something to say, say it."

The men stayed silent. Behind them, the television was spurting out baseball nonsense.

Shotgun Man put one hand on the door and stopped. He smelt that pancake aroma again. "God, I need to eat." He walked out of the bar, leaving those baseball assholes behind. So what if he didn't get the job done? He'd get it done eventually. Besides, there was something strange about the whole thing and if the bosses didn't like it, then they could come down to the bar and look for Johnny Balance themselves.

There was a diner across the street so Shotgun Man walked over to it, hoping to get some pancakes to satisfy his sudden craving. As he entered the place, there was no smell of flapjacks or any other food. There was only the stench of alcohol.

He walked up to the counter and made eye contact with a woman who was wearing a nametag that said her name was Cathy. She slowly walked over to him and said, "What can I get for you?"

"You have pancakes?" Shotgun Man said.

"Sure do," she said. "Want a short stack or regular stack?"

"Regular."

"Anything else?"

"No."

"You sure? We have farm fresh eggs."

"Just pancakes."

Cathy walked away and went into the kitchen. Shotgun Man looked around and saw that all of the other patrons were quietly sitting at their tables with no food in front of them. He thought that was strange. Could it be that the cook was so slow that no orders had gotten out yet?

Shotgun Man put his hands on the counter and leaned forward, trying to get a look into the kitchen. As soon as he did so, he felt something dig into his back. He turned his head quickly and received a fist to the eye.

His gun was pulled out of his jacket by an unseen hand and another fist slammed into his temple. The sudden attack disoriented him and Shotgun man found himself more confused than he had ever been. He caught a glimpse of the person who was hitting him. It was Cathy.

Now she had a gun to his cheek. She said, "You think you're gonna come in here and kill my son and I'm just going to sit back and let it happen? Huh?"

"What? What do you mean?" Shotgun Man said. He was sincerely confused and that prevented him from making any sort of move. It was as if all of his skills had been erased from his mind. "Your son? Who's your son?"

"Like you don't know, squid-fucker," she said. "Like you aren't looking for Johnny."

Shotgun Man shrugged. "Yes, I'm looking for him."

"So you could kill him?"

"Yes. So I could kill him." The gun dug deeper into his cheek.

"I'm his mother. What do you think I should do? Huh?"

"Whatever you have to," Shotgun Man said. "Right now, I can't do a thing about it and I don't know why."

Cathy smiled. "You smell pancakes, don't you?"

"Yes. I do."

The waitress laughed, taking the gun away from his face and then sticking it under his chin. "You can't move, huh?"

"No."

"Well, you won't be able to kill my son, then, huh?"

"Guess not."

Cathy twisted the gun. "Where're you from, anyway?"

"Chicago."

"No, I mean, what country. You have an accent."

Shotgun Man grimaced. Everyone in America always wanted to know where someone is from as if that really made a difference in matters of life and death.

He said, "Sicily."

Cathy grunted. "Heard it's nice over there."

"It is."

"They have pancakes in Sicily?"

"What kind of question is that?"

"It's just a question," she said. "Just a question."

Cathy shook her head and pulled the trigger. The top of Shotgun Man's head flipped open like a can of tuna fish. Grey matter and bloodied skull peppered the ceiling. His body fell to the floor, dirtying the linoleum.

The customers in the diner stared at Cathy and the corpse without emotion.

A young man walked out of the kitchen and stood next to Cathy. He said, "Mom, I could've handled him myself, you know."

Cathy slammed the gun on the counter. "Really, Johnny? If you could have handled it yourself, why didn't you kill those other squid-fuckers when you had the chance?"

"I had problems, ma," Johnny said. "You know I have emotional issues."

"Yeah, I know. That's all I've been hearing about for years," Cathy said. She grabbed Shotgun Man's legs and started to pull him. "Now help me dump this asshole and then go back to making those pancakes. We got hungry customers."

"Okay, ma," Johnny said, grabbing one of Shotgun Man's legs. "You think maybe later I could take the car and go over to Peggy's?"

Cathy stopped dragging the corpse and stared at her son. "Are you kidding me, Johnny? After all this, you expect to see that whore again? Let me tell you something. You're staying home tonight. You're staying home with me and we're going to watch the game."

"The game? Who's playing, ma?"

"Phillies, I think. But that doesn't really matter, does it?"

"No, guess not."

"Anyway, that's not all we're doing, Johnny. Tonight, I'm going to teach you a few things about life."

"Life?"

"Yeah, life," Cathy said. "And if you're lucky, maybe death, too."

APPENDIX IV
PINK MEAT RISING

Long lines of red dust create faces that signal me forward to encounter symmetrical genitals full of pox. There are bellies full of mental viruses and rumbling concrete bowels that tell me so many filthy words.

I shoplifted a book, several books actually. I read them in the parking lot. I learned about magick and crime, sigils for extortion. You know, tough guy stuff, all of which made me into the man I am today.

Victorian devils once gathered at the foot of my bed, spilling their seed in spirals of lust. I experienced fevers of apocalypse toy donkeys. I fear that someday they'll bring me to the hospital and I won't be leaving.

Sifting through dime store alibis for a beast of burden while belching symbols of redemption, I think of my Uncle Timothy and his box full of hair. Every strand was a vile story that demanded to be told to all who would listen.

We ride into town to rob banks and cast spells with shotguns. We are blood-spilling bastards in debt. There's something special about smoking cigarettes in hiding and counting unmarked bills. It makes me feel at home. Then I remember I have to dig a hole and throw the guns in.

Mentally ill squid eating brains of crime, forcing eyes to stare at bags of teeth and large breasted viruses. I give myself up to black magick bowel movements. I've read this book five, maybe six times and I still don't understand the ending. There was something about pancakes, something about death, squid, and a desire to sink one's teeth into smelly shoe leather.

Enough with the fucking squid already.

We've gathered plastic bags full of fever. My throat is a dustpan where illness is expected. Sometimes I wish it wasn't worshipped. Old red gods pick apart my immune system until I'm coughing up pictures of whores who will destroy me in the world to come.

Goddamn those sweet cheeks luring me in until I can't resist. I gorge myself on the snakes in your abdomen. Morning comes and its all stained fingers and sore teeth. A girl wakes up beside me, looking like a pale queen, holding flowers against her chest, weeds jutting up from her ample cleavage. I hear the voice of my father telling me to mow the lawn, mow the lawn.

Mow the lawn.

Around the room there are symbols of a world flushed with blood. My bowels are ready to fall like an empire. We should've been on the road an hour ago. There are bloody holes and clumps of hair everywhere. Where the hell are the car keys? Where's my wallet?

There is no universal truth that doesn't involve visions of blue teeth and pink meat. Soft stars chew me up as I ride on currents of menstrual runes. I'll be engulfed in squid-like flames that pick at the scabs of apocalypse, forcing me to accept that the assassination was real and not just a bloody puppet show.

We'll both witness the blue light of Lincoln and of Christ as we get into the car and speed down highways of apple crepes and blueberry rape. Blackbirds will babble about the green breath of God and his assassins. Where are our families now? Where is the safety net of tradition? Decades mean nothing when there is no past, no future.

The car is making a weird noise. Turn the radio up to drown it out. No, I don't care what station you put on.

Signs up ahead will tell us to turn left. We always turn left.

But there will be nothing left.

ABOUT THE AUTHOR

Jordan Krall is the author of several books including PIECEMEAL
JUNE, SQUID PULP BLUES, and FISTFUL OF FEET. His work has
been praised by such authors as Edward Lee and Tom Piccirilli.
Jordan divides his time between New Jersey, Nevada, and Tibet.

Readers, reviewers, and fans of Italian exploitation movies are
encouraged to contact him at www.filmynoir.com.

*"It has been my experience that folks who have no vices have very
little virtues."*

Abraham Lincoln